The Lions Fed the Tigers

The Lions Fed

HOUGHTON MIFFLIN COMPANY

the Tigers

BY DOUGLAS ANGUS

with decorations by PETER SPIER

BOSTON · The Riverside Press Cambridge · 1958

FIRST PRINTING

LIBRARY OF CONGRESS CATALOG CARD NUMBER: 58-9051

The Riverside Press
CAMBRIDGE • MASSACHUSETTS
PRINTED IN THE U.S.A.

to my father and mother

The Lions Fed the Tigers

I

In the big house on Clifford Street the old man upstairs coughed all day and coughed all night. It didn't bother Ian any more than a cricket in the wall, but it was bad for his father's insomnia. So for that and bad business generally his father decided to move to the Dodd's Block, a four-family tenement in the center of town, where the trappers coming in from the railroad station would have to pass the sign in the parlor window: Wallace McAleenan Dealer in Hides and Raw Furs. Uncle Rufus said it wouldn't help a bit. This whole damn section was dead — left high and dry, all the money drained away into the big cities by the big insurance companies. That was the real curse of the land — the big insurance companies. There were good times before they appeared on the scene. The only thing to do was move out to the country and raise enough to eat and let it go at that. As to making an extra dollar at any kind of honest business, well, look at the shoe factory. No human being could have done more than he had to make it pay, and after all his efforts the big city manufacturers had cut his throat, and now there was the factory like a cliff, casting its shadow over the whole town, and here was he — bankrupt — down and out, ruined at fifty, and the whole town ruined with him, everybody looking at him reproachfully if he took a walk along a street. If they moved to the Dodd's Block, he'd have to wake up every morning and see the factory from the back door, and he'd just as soon wake up with a morning view of the old pit itself.

But his father went ahead anyway, even though the week before they moved, the old man gave a big cough, a little cough, and passed away. They put him in a coffin in the parlor, where he lay like an old man of chalk in the smell of the flowers and the green light of the drawn blinds. It was surprising how many flowers were sent by people who hadn't visited the old man for years.

To Ian it was all quite magnificent — the old man's dying a mystery of mysteries, and riding across town on top of the load of furniture, with the kitchen table on its back like an upset bug, the bureau mirror wobbling, and the kitchen stovepipe thrust out over the town like a cannon, was almost too wonderful to be real. He only wished he had a bugle to blow as he rode along.

And there was the Dodd's Block, like a giant boot box, with its flat roof that was always leaking so that men came with long ladders and buckets of tar to stand astride on the roof edge calling down from the sky. What a fascinating place with its four blistered purple doors, its narrow bay windows and four identical woodsheds in the back. Behind it was the yard, an incredible jungle of wooden platforms, sheds on top of sheds, shadowy passageways, clotheslines and high fences — a land of Canaan, so that it made no sense at all the way his father's forehead wrinkled or his mother's mouth tightened when she looked out of the kitchen window of their new home.

But then they didn't seem to know about the Antonellis, who lived in the next apartment. Ian knew all about them. When he put his ear to the wall he could hear them moving and breathing like a many-voiced animal. There was no other family like the Antonellis. Mr. Antonelli ran a little restaurant. He was Italian, short and swarthy, with a thick mustache and bright black eyes. Mrs. Antonelli was English and very beautiful. They had four daughters. There was something wonderful going on in the Antonelli apartment, something foreign and strange, something bright and boisterous, like a band concert, and never ending. It began in the morning, when Mr. Antonelli woke up with a mighty yawn that was half groan and half roar of rage. What woke up Mr. Antonelli and everybody else in the Dodd's Block was Ian's father down in his woodshed chopping kindlings. His father always got up at dawn, and as if he held a spite against all the other people for being able to still sleep, immediately began to make as much noise as possible. Chopping wood in the woodshed was perfect for his purpose. Thunder and cannon could not have made more noise.

"The devil take that man and his infernal chopping!" Mr. Antonelli would exclaim. Then there would come a murmur from Mrs. Antonelli and after a while a sharp smack that would be Mr. Antonelli giving her a slap on the backside — the way he did every time he passed her in the yard. It seemed he just couldn't pass Mrs. Antonelli's backside without giving it a slap — only in the bedroom it was her *bare* backside that he slapped. Ian could hear everything through the thin wall.

After the smack would come a long silence. Then Mr. Antonelli would say, "I think I will." And sometimes there would be another long silence, but usually Mrs. Antonelli would laugh and say, "I guess you won't." Then Mr. Antonelli would groan and say it was a curse of Satan to be married to such a stubborn and beautiful woman. And Mrs. Antonelli would call him an old goat — it was always an old goat — and ask him if he wanted another daughter. About that time there would come a banging on their bedroom door, and it would be Constantia, or Maria, or Olivia, but never Francesca, the oldest, shouting for their breakfasts.

"Go away," would cry Mr. Antonelli. "I'm asleep."

Then the door would fly open and all three, Constantia, Maria, and Olivia, would burst into the room with a wild whoop, and the bed would creak and groan, and Mr. Antonelli would cry out, "Help, help. Save me from all this woman!" And such a noise would go out through the open window that everybody was sure to know that the Antonellis were awake and the day had begun.

It was a puzzle — the Antonellis and their happiness. He thought it must all come from Mrs. Antonelli with her great shining eyes and her face as smooth and white as melting ice cream, who lifted up his chin with her hand the first time she saw him and asked him if he didn't think his mother would trade him for one of her girls. "I think I'll let Constantia go," she had said. "She's the bad one." And Constantia, looking worried for a moment, had caught her mother's eye and had broken into a wide-mouthed happy grin.

The Van Eppses, in the far apartment, were quite different. Little Mr. Van Epps coming home from his cobbler's shop never seemed to look up. If you spoke to him he mumbled something in his strange accent that was completely unintelligible, even though he repeated everything three times out of habit. In the evening he sat polishing the little brass ornaments on the mantel, ornaments brought over from Holland, and drinking the beer he made once a month in the washtub and poured into stone bottles with wooden stoppers that clamped down tight with wires.

Mrs. Van Epps seemed to be forever standing in her doorway calling her two children in from the yard. "Ermin—ee! Hen—ree!" first note low, second note shrill as a steam whistle. "I'll give you a smack now!"

And a smack they always got. She smacked them as they scooted past her, their little heads down between their shoulders. She smacked them as they scurried through the woodshed. She smacked them up to the kitchen sink to be washed—with carbolic soap—and she smacked them into place at the supper table. Smack! Smack! Left ear—right ear, she pursued them furiously through the house, until Ian, watching hypnotized, wondered if she wasn't going to give Mr. Van Epps one of her hard smacks, too, as he sat silently by the kitchen stove staring at his shoes. Little Henry walked with a permanent crick in his neck from wincing under that hard, merciless hand, stepping along softly on his toes as if he were walking on thin ice. But Erminie was different. Her head bobbed up straight as ever, as soon as she was out of her mother's reach. But Erminie never laughed. Her rosy face under the flaxen hair was cast in a perpetual scowl, her eyes stormy and brooding.

But there was a mystery about humble Mr. Van Epps. The mystery was in the way Ian's father and his Uncle Rufus always spoke to Mr. Van Epps with a very special tone of respect. One day, after they had just passed Mr. Van Epps, his uncle said to him, "Did you notice that little man?"

He nodded.

"You wouldn't guess that he is a master craftsman, one of the world's best shoe designers. He designed the Forshay shoe — the best damn shoe ever made in Canada."

Ian turned to look at the little gray figure hurrying home to his cross wife.

"And what's he doing?" Uncle Rufus' voice rose. "Cobbling! Mending old shoes! It's a crime — I tell you!" He walked on, shaking his head and thrusting out his arm the way he always did when he was aroused, as if he had once worn a coat with the sleeves too long.

Between the Antonellis and the Van Eppses lived Mrs. McCracken with the three oval portraits of her sons killed in the World War. It was like an empty apartment.

The first morning, Ian came out the back door and stared across the yard at the fantastic architecture of the Moylan Apartments — at the upper woodsheds resting on posts on top of the lower woodsheds, at the gloomy passageways, the endless little black holes with doors that swung outward, where the face of one of the old Moylan sisters might pop out at any moment, at the coal-loading platform, to which the truckman had to toss up the coal and then stand on to toss it into one of the little openings. He wet his lips. If ever a building had been constructed for climbing, this was it.

Uncle Rufus stepped out for his morning constitutional, stared up at the Moylan Apartments, said, "My God!" and went off up the yard.

A small boy with very large, limpid brown eyes and a pointed little face came out of the shadows, crossed the yard and climbed up on the high whitewashed fence at the end. Ian followed him.

"Want to go to the store with me?" the boy said, looking down at him.

Ian was wary. "What store?"

"B.J.'s."

"That's the other way."

The boy didn't comment. "My name's Ely," he said. He pointed toward the house on the other side of the fence. "That's where the spider lives."

Ian crawled up beside him. "What spider?" he asked.

"Old Mrs. Gallup, the spider."

Ian stared at the little gray house almost buried under vines. Vines grew all over the roof and down the sides, around the windows, and hung in festoons from the eaves of the back porch. They even went out along the clothesline to the fence on which they were perched.

"Why is she a spider?"

"Watch." Ely gave one of the vines a violent jerk. Immediately, as if by magic, a wrinkled old face flashed at one of the festooned windows and a sharp rat-a-tat sounded on the glass. "See — just like a spider." Ely rubbed his nose. "The thing to do is to get across her yard and up over the other fence before she gets you with her stick." He gave Ian an appraising look. "Wanta try it?"

Ian looked at the little house. "Where do you think she is now?"

"Right behind the door, waiting."

"All right."

"Ya gotta grab a couple of her peonies to make her real mad." Ely stood up, balanced a moment, and jumped fair into the middle of the peony bed. He grabbed two of the white blooms and tore across the yard. Halfway over he stopped. "Come on!" he cried.

For just an instant longer Ian hesitated, then leaped. At that moment Ely let out a treacherous yell at the top of his lungs and streaked for the far fence. Ian grabbed two blooms, took three steps across the yard, and leaped like a gazelle as the back door flew back against the wall and old Mrs. Gallup came scuttling across the yard after him, her cane waving in the air, her face livid with rage. Desperately he scrambled up the high fence on the other side of the yard, where Ely crouched like a squirrel and stared down at him with cool, interested eyes. He got up all right, but not before the cane whistled once against his backside. "Hoodlum! hoodlum! hoodlum!" shrieked old Mrs. Gallup.

By that time Ely had leaped to safety onto the big pile

of manure that crept up the side of the Brander Livery Stable. Ian teetered on top of the fence, staring down at the fearsome pool of horse urine and stale water directly beneath. He gritted his teeth and jumped.

"That was a pretty good jump," Ely said as they walked down the side of the manure pile, completely ignoring old Mrs. Gallup, who was peering at them through the slats of the fence and wheezing threats of the police.

They stood outside of the livery stable. "You want to go in there?" Ely nodded toward the big barn.

Ian studied the pale, ratlike little face. He already had a healthy distrust of Ely, but he detected a dare in his voice. "Sure," he said.

"All right, but you got to be careful. Old man Brander won't let any boys near his stable; he's afraid they'll set it on fire. If he catches you, he'll stick a pitchfork into you as quick as wink." He studied Ian speculatively. "Come on," he said after a moment, "there's only one way to get in without being seen."

He led the way to a side door that opened into a cave-like cellar full of old buggies. They climbed onto one of the padded seats. "This is a good place to come to on a rainy day because of all the comfortable seats," Ely said.

"Is this as far as we go?" asked Ian.

Ely tilted his head, listening for footsteps above. After a moment he jumped from the buggy seat and led the way to the darkest corner of the cellar, where he stuck his head into a black opening. "You got sneakers on?" he asked pulling his head out again.

"Yes."

"You can't go up without sneakers. The sides are too slippery." He hesitated. "You wanta go first?"

"No thanks," said Ian.

Ely looked at him. "All right," he said, and as if he were afraid he might change his mind, he crawled at once through the black hole and began wriggling up the smooth sides of the chute. A few seconds later his voice whispered reassuringly down, and Ian started up after him. It was pitch-black inside and the sides were worn smooth as glass. He forced his way upward by bracing his back against one side and pushing the rubber soles of his sneakers hard against the other. It seemed to him that he had been struggling upward for a tremendously long time, when all at once he heard a yell like a thunderclap.

"So ho! Trying to sneak into my barn again!" A heavy object clattered against a wall somewhere above, and the next instant with a wild scrambling down came Ely, and the *next* instant their legs had become tangled and they were wedged fast, chest to chest, panting into each other's faces. "Ohmygod!" exclaimed Ely, "we're stuck!"

They wriggled and twisted and squirmed; it was no use.

A flashlight went on above their heads. They looked up at the round yellow disk. "Well, what do you know about that?" came a harsh voice from behind the light, "we've caught a couple of little rats down here in the chute. What do you think we ought to do with them?"

"Turn the hose on em," came a muffled voice from the horse stalls. "Drown the little bastards!"

"Ohmygod!" panted Ely. He gave a terrific twist of his body and without warning they both shot down the chute and out the opening, landing in a heap on the earth. They had hardly staggered to their feet when they heard the heavy spray of water hit the sides of the chute. They looked at each other and blinked.

"How do you like that?" yelled a voice above the sound of the water. "I guess you won't come sneaking around here smoking cigarettes any more for a while! Eh! What do you say? Ho ho ho ho!"

Ely leaned down by the opening. "Go stick your head in a bucket, old crumpet face!" he yelled.

There was a sudden silence above. They turned and walked leisurely over to the window of the barn cellar and crawled outside.

Beyond them was the warehouse of the Eastern Hay and

Feed Co., with about thirty enormous puncheons lying about on their sides or ends. Ely ran ahead sniffing at the bungholes. Every time he sniffed he stuck his head up and cried, "Kerosene!" or "Vinegar," keeping it up until at last he found what he was looking for and yelled triumphantly, "Molasses!"

They heaved the big puncheon up until it was tipped on its rim, and while Ian held it that way, Ely caught on his finger some of the thick, black, odorous syrup that came trickling out of the hole. When his finger was well covered he stuck it into his mouth, closing his eyes and smacking his lips loudly.

Ian didn't care much for either the smell or the look of the stuff as it oozed out of the bung; moreover, a big fly buzzed out just as he took his finger away. But under Ely's watchful eye he sucked his finger clean and smacked his lips with enthusiasm. It tasted a little bit like something his mother used to give him for the spring sickness.

They ran then, leaping from one wobbly puncheon to another until they reached the far side of the yard and were standing at last before the partly opened back door of the grocery store. Ely peered into the back shop, his eyes darting this way and that among the stacks of cartons, boxes and barrels.

"There's always something you can pick up in here," he whispered. "The last time there was an open crate of oranges." He glance at Ian over his shoulder. "You slip in. I'll watch here to see nobody comes."

"Huh," said Ian. "Slip in yourself."

"All right. If you're scared, we'll go in together."

They crawled up over the high door sill. "You go over and watch by the door to the front part," Ely said, "and I'll see what I can find."

Ian crept toward the door. It was slightly ajar, and peering through the crack he saw his Uncle B.J. standing by the scales holding a scoop of sugar over a paper bag. He glanced back at Ely, who was darting about ducking into barrels, prying at the tops of crates, reaching into bags, for all the world like a lively, industrious little mouse. Ian turned back to the door. His uncle was leaning over the counter talking to a stout lady. "Yes," he was saying. "I've just got some in. They're out in the back shop — "

Ian didn't wait to hear more, but turned and dashed for the back door. Ely swung around, his eyes questioning. He had both hands down in a barrel, and when he came leaping toward the door after Ian he held a great gob of something in either hand, something that dripped as he ran.

"This way," he hissed. "There isn't time to make it across the yard." Darting down he scooted right in under the back shop. Ian followed on his hands and knees, scrambling after him over the dry straw to the darkest corner, where they lay breathing hard and listening to B.J. walking around over their heads.

"What did you get?" Ian asked. His mouth was already watering at the thought of juicy ripe bananas, chocolate-covered marshmallow cookies, or even a handful of chocolate bars.

Ely held up his hands. "This is all I could find open — sauerkraut." He held out a handful.

Ian peered at the sour-smelling stuff. He could still taste the fermented molasses in his mouth. He nibbled cautiously.

But Ely shoved it down recklessly, sitting in the dark on his haunches, chewing steadily, his brown eyes glittering. He looked more like a mouse than ever. "See why I came to the store this way?" he said. "I once swiped a whole baloney from the back shop and ate it right down to the end, while B.J. walked around over my head looking for it."

After a while they crawled out and went around to the front of the store, where Ely went in and bought the package of tapioca his mother had sent him for.

As they walked up the street, the whistle of the coffin factory blew noon. It was the only factory whistle left, the only business that flourished in the depression — making coffins. As Uncle Rufus said, if it wasn't for the coffins the town would be really dead. But coffin makers and undertakers were always prosperous, good times and bad. The trouble was, people would patch and mend their shoes, but everybody wanted a brand new coffin.

"You got any money?" Ely asked abruptly.

Ian shook his head.

"Want to make some?"

"You can't make money in this town," Ian said, quoting his Uncle Rufus. "You can't get honey from grasshoppers."

Ely wrinkled the end of his sharp nose. "*I* can," he said.

"How?"

"I'll show you after supper. Even I can't make money until after supper." As he spoke Ely vaulted the low place in the fence and turned into a fourteen-inch alley between the Moylan Apartments and the house where he lived with his grandfather and grandmother.

In the evening, when the stars were flecks of tinsel in the pale green sky, and the night hawks were just beginning to swoop over their heads, the two boys walked down Albion Street, turned in the alley between B.J.'s store and the warehouse, and came to a ten-foot-high picket fence. "There you are," said Ely.

Ian peered through the slats at a weird landscape of old auto frames, wagon wheels, broken farm machinery, stoves, a couple of huge, rusty old boilers, metal tubs, pots — in fact everything made out of iron was there in some stage of dilapidation.

"Old man Mooney's junk yard," Ely said. "You want a wheel for a cart, or a set of handlebars, it's in there. All you gotta do is find it. Come on." He walked along the fence until he came to a place where four spikes were driven inconspicuously into the fence and was suddenly up and over the high slats like a cat. Looking around once, Ian followed.

"All day old Mooney sits in his door watching his junk, but at night he goes home." Ely bent over, picked up an iron kettle and threw it over the fence.

"What are you doing?" Ian asked.

"Getting junk." Ely tossed a stove lid over the fence.

"You mean *stealing* junk."

Ely straightened up. His voice sounded hurt. "This junk don't belong to nobody."

"It belongs to old Mooney."

Ely waggled his head. "Old Mooney just owns a quarter of it. The rest don't belong to nobody."

"Huh!" said Ian.

"It's the truth. Mooney pays a cent a pound for it, and it's worth five cents a pound. Everybody knows that. So I don't see how he owns more than a quarter of it. So come on. Lend a hand."

Ian scratched his head. It sounded very convincing. He picked up a piece of pipe and threw it over the fence.

In the morning they marched around to old Mooney's office with their plunder over their shoulders in two potato bags. Mooney was sitting at his desk and swung around in his broken swivel chair. His fat legs stuck straight out in front of him, and his little eyes glittered. "Vere you gat dis stuff?" he wheezed.

"Aah! We get it here and there." Ely leaned against the wall picking his teeth.

"Oh ho! You gat it here and dere huh? You mean you gat it in dis town huh?"

"Sure we got it in this town."

"Vell." Mooney leaned a little forward, and the old chair tilting brought his stubby feet down to the floor. "Dere aint any junk left in dis town. Everybody sold deir junk." He waved his short arms. "Dere's none left — not a rusty nail — not a hairpin. So — " he rubbed his bristly jowl — "I don know where you gat dis stuff." He peered suspiciously at the heap of scrap on the floor. "It looks a lot like wat I gut in de yard." His eyes glittered up at them momentarily.

Ely looked insulted.

"Ten cents."

Ely looked shocked. "You want to rob us?" he said.

"All right. All right. Twelf cents. Throw it ofer on de pile." Old Mooney apparently never moved unless he had to. He made his customers do all the work.

So they went into the junk business. For two weeks they sold old Mooney his own junk daily, but each time he looked surlier than ever, until one day he actually pulled himself out of his swivel chair, grabbed a stove leg and waved it violently under their noses. "I already haf bought dis stove leg from you last week!" he yelled. "You tink I don know my own stove leg!"

"Mr. Mooney!" Ely drew himself up. "As a member of the Presbyterian Church I solemnly swear you never owned that stove leg."

Mooney stopped waving the stove leg under Ely's chin. "You belong to da Presbyterian Church?"

"I take the communion."

"Vel — " Mooney lowered the stove leg. "In dat case — "

"We gotta be careful we don't sell him that stove leg four times," Ely said as they walked up the street, "because then he would really own it. I wouldn't want to rob the old fellow."

"Me neither," Ian said.

But the next evening as they came up to the junk yard,

they heard an ominous growling from the other side of the fence, and there sniffing and snorting at them through the slats was surely the ugliest beast that man had ever invented, a great white bulldog with a mouth like a trap door to the Inferno, all fangs and red tongue. Ely thrust a stick through the slats and watched the beast gnash it into matchwood. "Well, there goes our business," he said disconsolately.

For several days following, whenever they passed his shop, Mooney would take the trouble to heave himself out of his chair and come out onto the front platform, from where he would call to them, "Vat is de matter? You are not getting any junk dese days?" And he would give a great throaty laugh and turn back into his shop.

It was a bitter pill to swallow. For days they racked their brains for some solution. Evening after evening they strolled down to the junk-yard fence, but the dog was always there sniffing and growling. They tried to make friends with him, calling him pet names through the slats. He only growled the more fiercely. They threw water at him, but he only shook his great head leaving long drools of saliva hanging from the slats. They threw sticks and stones at him, but these just bounced off his leathery hide.

It was Ian who finally got the idea of trying pepper. He brought a full package down from his mother's pantry, and when the big dog's snout came sniffing between the slats, he let him have the whole thing right in his red drooling mouth. For a split second there was silence, the big dog paralyzed with surprise, then a single ear-piercing howl shattered the sky, and whirling on his short legs he shot off like a dirty gray streak for the shelter under the back steps of the shop, where he tore at his nose with his paws, yelping and snorting and peering out at them from red-rimmed, terrified eyes.

The next evening they arrived fortified with a second supply of pepper, but no sooner had they come in sight than the dog tore for his refuge under the steps as if the devil of all dogs was after him.

But tossing pepper at him and getting inside the fence were two different things. They stared uncomfortably at each other. Alone Ian would never have found the courage to do such a crazy thing, but with Ely watching him he somewhere found the courage, and in a moment was moving cautiously through the junk yard, pepper box in one hand, his eye on the dog peeking at him from under the steps and growling like all the demons of hell, but never budging. Quickly Ian picked up the nearest pieces of iron and tossed them over the fence. And when he was finally safely back on the other side of the fence, he felt a little bigger, and walked with a little swagger for a while.

Old Mooney had hardly opened the shop the next morning before they appeared with their booty. Silently, he stared at the little pile of scrap, silently his small eyes traveled over their faces, silently he waved toward the scales, and silently he tossed the few coins at their feet. When they looked back from the doorway, he was still sitting there, looking at the bits of iron at his feet. It was one of life's big moments.

From then on he paid them without a murmur. But there was always a haunted look in his eyes, like a man who is feeling in his pocket for his wallet and can't find it. One day, when they stepped into his shop, he was holding the old bulldog on a leash. No sooner had they stepped inside than the dog took one look at them, gave a mighty jerk so sudden that it toppled old Mooney, chair and all, over onto the floor, and shot like a bolt for the open back door. For several seconds old Mooney just sat there, his short legs still up in the air, his back against a pile of old burlap sacks, his eyes moving from the open door through which the dog had vanished to their blank faces and back again. The expression on his face was a sight to remember.

That evening when Ian's mother sat down at the supper table she looked at him hard. "There's something strange going on in this house," she said.

"If you want to kill a fly that's on the butter, you do it like this," said Uncle Rufus. He held his hands out on either side of the butter, then clapped them together just above the butter. The fly flew up, was neatly killed between Uncle Rufus' hands and fell down into the butter dish.

"As I said." His mother picked the dead fly out of the butter. "There's something queer going on here. I bought a new package of pepper last week and today when I looked for it it was gone."

"Tut, tut," his father said. "You just *thought* you bought a new package of pepper last week."

"I *know* I bought it," his mother said coldly. She looked again at Ian. "You couldn't possibly have any use for pepper in your affairs, could you, Ian?"

He turned over a piece of meat with his fork. "What on earth would I be doing with pepper?" he said.

"I can't imagine." She was silent for a moment. "But I certainly can't imagine what your father would be doing with it."

His father looked up startled. "Pepper?" he said. "Are you accusing me of going to your pantry and stealing off with the pepper?"

"Never mind," his mother said in a tired voice. "I'll just buy another package. Sometimes I think my mind is going."

"If everybody will keep quiet for a moment, I'll say the blessing," his father said. They folded their hands and stared at their plates. "For what we are about to receive, the Lord make us truly thankful — and help us to be true Christians — " His father's voice dropped to a solemn whisper, "For Christ's sake, amen!"

They began to eat.

2

UNCLE RUFUS stopped rocking. "Now listen to this." He moved his finger along the page. "In many sections of Africa the Negroes are beginning to wear shoes, a fact which may revitalize the entire shoe industry. On this dark continent there are fifty million Negroes who have never known the safety and comfort of shoes. Here is a market whose potential we can only guess — Here — "

Ian's father put his newspaper down. "Rufus, Rufus!" he exclaimed. "When are you going to stop dreaming about that old factory?"

Uncle Rufus thrust out his arm. "I can't get it out of my head that it's there. The machinery and all, as good as the day it was built."

"It would take five hundred dollars just to replace the broken windows," his father said.

"I remember when we built it." Uncle Rufus stared off into the distance. "We thought that with cheap fuel from the soft-coal mines and our central location —"

"Central location!" Ian's father scoffed. "Where did we ever get the idea we had a central location? Actually, we are away the devil off to nowhere. Central location ha!"

But Uncle Rufus hardly seemed to hear him. "There was something in the air then," he muttered. "I don't know what it was. The world looked different. Things seemed possible."

Ian's mother looked up. "You were young then, Rufus. That's all." She smiled on him tenderly.

"No," his father said. "It's simply that times have changed. We're in a depression. Rufus knows it. We all know it. You'll see I won't do any better here with my hides than I did on Clifford Street. I don't know why I moved. I don't sleep any better here, that's certain."

Ian got up and went out. He felt all bottled up. He stood on the front steps and drew in a long breath. The evening was clear and crisp; an absolutely pure band of brilliant lemon yellow lay to the west. Suddenly the energy locked up inside him became insistent. He ran down the walk, turned and began to run fast down the street. He pulled his elbows in against his ribs, and he fairly drove his feet against the cinder sidewalk. Faster and faster he went. It was like magic; his feet in his sneakers seemed to have wings. There was no effort. He turned and tore down Douglas Avenue. A man standing in front of a house called out, "Where's the fire?"

He ran all the way around the block and then sat

down on the front steps with his whole body glowing and trembling. I could be a champion long distance runner, he thought.

He and Ely picked up a new friend, a boy named Peebles, with a big Adam's apple and hair the color of a Rhode Island Red rooster. He didn't believe in anything when they met him and began every remark with "Aw!" They had to prove everything for him, so he was a kind of stimulus. They took him into the junk business, which was flourishing.

One afternoon they went over to the old shoe factory.

"This factory used to belong to my Uncle Rufus," Ian said casually.

Ely stared up at the big building. "*That* belonged to your uncle?" he asked incredulously.

Ian nodded. They looked at him with a new respect.

"Who owns it now?" Peebles asked.

"The bank owns it now." Ian shrugged.

They were sitting in a patch of sunlight by the Eastern Hay and Feed warehouse trying out a new kind of cigarette made out of tea and toilet paper. The smell was horrible, but as the advertisements said, they were "easier on the throat — " easier, that is, than the string ones they *had* been smoking.

"All my life I been wanting to see the inside of that old factory," Ely said. "The way they got it locked up you'd think it was full of diamonds or something."

"If we had one of those Big Berthas the Germans used, we could just blow a hole in the side and walk in." Peebles coughed, looking at his cigarette as if it had bitten him.

"If you hit this old factory with a Big Bertha," Ely said, "the whole thing would fall down."

"No it wouldn't," Ian said.

Peebles was staring thoughtfully at the long shed across the alley from the factory wall. "If we had a plank," he said, "we could push it across from that shed roof to one of those second story windows and crawl across."

"I don't see any planks around here," Ely said.

Ian glanced down. "We're sittin on a plank," he said.

Somehow they got the plank up on the shed roof. It was too heavy to push out to the window, but they solved that difficulty by standing it on end and letting it fall. The third time it fell just right, its end landing on the window sill. One after the other they crawled across, and at last were inside the factory.

It was kind of like a church, Ian thought. Everywhere were the ghostly shapes of machines covered with a thin mantle of dust. From the high windows came long gashes of pale yellow sunlight. Speaking in whispers they tiptoed along between the machines with their maze of belts and chains.

Ian hung back. He ran his fingers over the machines. Under the thin coating of grease they were smooth and shiny. He had a dim memory of being in the factory just once, long ago, when he was very little, when all the machines were running. He remembered the clatter and flashing of wheels. He looked down the length of the interior. Once his Uncle Rufus had said that if all the machines in the factory were running again, the whole town would come alive. The men on the street would walk quickly, and Uncle B.J. and his father would all straighten up and become cheerful.

He followed the others into a curious little room with ropes running up and down the walls, and a floor that quivered under their feet. In one corner was a small pile of shoeboxes and in them some shoes — but what shoes! high-topped shoes of black patent leather with buttons. They were all down on the floor buttoning their feet into these ludicrous shoes when they heard a creaking sound and looking up saw to their amazement and fright that the floor outside the room was slowly rising to the ceiling. Then the truth dawned on them. They were in the elevator.

They held their breaths, but their fear changed to sheer joy, as slowly and serenely they floated down past the first floor, down into the dark basement. They sat on the elevator in their button shoes and grinned at each other. What an adventure!

They wondered how they could get it to go up again. They jiggled the ropes in vain. Then Peebles stepped off in disgust, and at once the elevator started floating up again like a veritable balloon. Gaily they sailed up and up, while the frustrated wails of Peebles came to them from below. Past the first floor, the second floor, the third floor, and past the fourth and last floor they rose. They stared at each other. How was it possible? There were only four floors. But before they could figure it out, the elevator crashed against the top of the shaft, and opening a door they found themselves nowhere but on the roof itself of the shoe factory. Gingerly they stepped out onto the expanse of flat, tar-covered surface. There, spread out before their eyes like a picture map, was the whole town. There was the big gray Catholic Church, and the smaller Presbyterian tower with the clock. There was the round silver plate of Christie's Pond. They could even see the junk yard, with old Mooney poking about, and old Mr. Cotter sitting in front of his tinsmith shop taking the sun.

"Look!" Ian pointed excitedly. "There's Mrs. Van Epps hanging out her wash."

"Jeepers!" Ely cried suddenly. He was staring at the clock on the town hall. "It's six o'clock. I'm supposed to be home."

They ran for the elevator. "All aboard!" yelled Ely.

But the elevator didn't budge. They rocked it, they jumped up and down. It was no use. And it dawned on them that they were marooned — not on a desert island but on top of the shoe factory.

"Jumpin catfish!" Ely exclaimed. "They'll have to call out the fire department to get us down."

They walked around the roof looking for a trap door, but the only door they found was locked. Ian noticed a little pile of bricks near a skylight, and all at once he had one of his best ideas. He began to pick up an armload of bricks, and sure enough, when they both walked onto the elevator carrying as many bricks as they could lift, down it floated past floor after floor. Oh what fun on long rainy days to go floating up and floating down — as long as the

bricks on the roof lasted. "Oh the old shoe factory!" sang Ely. "She aint what she used to be — aint what she used to be." Ian joined in.

Suddenly in the midst of their song there came a ripping sound above their heads, a great snake of rope came curling down at them, and the next instant the elevator began to shoot down faster and faster. They shot past the first floor at a terrific clip, getting a quick glimpse of Peebles' frightened face. The next moment they crashed to the floor of the cellar with a jolt that shook every tooth in their heads.

HOTEL
TAYLOR
Y SOAP

Peebles' voice came quavering down. "Is anyone alive down there?"

"Naw," cried Ely. "We're dead, and I'm a ghost." He gave a long groan.

As they limped back, Ian stopped curiously by one of the machines — a sort of extra-large sewing machine. His eye had caught sight of the shoe still in the machine — an almost finished shoe. The long needle with the thread still there had gone down and had never come up again. Just a few more stitches on the tongue and the shoe would have been finished.

"Look at that," he said.

"Come on," Peebles exclaimed. "It's after six."

It wasn't until they had crossed the plank that they realized they were still wearing the button shoes. There was no time to go back.

"We can get our shoes in the morning," Ely said.

They walked along the alley in silence. "Do you suppose we can fix up that old elevator?" Ian said.

"Aw," Peebles said. "Do you want to break your neck forever?"

"Where in the name of heaven have you *been*?" Ian's mother said. "We finished supper ages ago."

"Oh just playing around the old shoe factory." He went over to the kitchen sink and turned the water on his dusty hands.

"You better keep away from that factory." His father's voice came from the parlor. "A loose brick might fall on your head."

His mother hung up the dish towel. "You'll find your

dinner in the warming oven." She turned to go into the parlor, then whirled about and stared at his feet. "What on earth," she cried, "have you got on your feet?"

He looked down and saw the high black button shoes in all their shiny splendor.

His mother started to laugh. "Oh! oh!" she cried, pressing her hand to her mouth. "They're just like the ones your father wore when he first came to call on me. I guess I've seen everything. Where did you dig up those — those monstrosities?"

He grinned sheepishly, searching frantically for some explanation.

"And where — " her voice was suddenly serious — "are your own shoes?"

"I traded em," he said quickly.

"Oh you *did!* Well first thing in the morning you go and trade them right back." She looked at the shoes and started to laugh again. "Wait till your father sees them. I bet they'll make him quite romantic again." She giggled softly as she went out of the room.

They picked up a couple of new friends. One was a gangly-limbed, freckle-faced boy called Dusty, who lived on Douglas Avenue in a drab little house full of plants. There was hardly room to move anywhere in the house because of the plants, and it was so dark you had to feel your way around for a chair. His mother was very proud of the plants, although Ian could never see why, for there was never a flower among them — just a great tangled mass of twisting stems and coarse leaves extending from floor to ceiling and cutting off what little light trickled through the small windows. The house had an odd musty smell.

Dusty walked with a peculiar, sway-backed motion that came from constantly trying to stick out his skinny chest. But he was a noble fellow. You couldn't help feeling his nobleness. He never smiled and was always talking about fair play and foul play. He was generous to a fault, for he insisted on sharing whatever he had, but would never accept a thing in return.

Dusty's ambition was to be a boxer. He knew all about boxing. He had picked up the history of it from the backs of the little pictures of former champions that came with certain chocolate bars. Whenever he had five cents he bought another chocolate bar, kept the picture and gave the candy away.

At the slightest provocation Dusty fell into the Dempsey crouch or the Fitzsimmons stance with one foot forward, or preferably a stance that he had invented himself, which was a crouch with the left arm extended as far as he could reach. "Wear em down with your left," he would say and proceed to give you a number of little taps on the chin that wouldn't have worn down a healthy fly. He was always doing road work to develop his leg muscles and his wind. If you got up early in the morning, you might see him loping along the empty street with his elbows close to his sides and his chin stuck out as if he couldn't quite catch up with it.

But Dusty was a great fellow. While Ely, one hundred per cent practical, was always the first to run in a tight spot, Dusty was on his honor to be the last; in fact, it seemed to hurt his feelings if anyone else tried to be as brave as he was. He was always a great asset whenever they seemed about to get into a fight with the French boys, who lived over on Fuller Street. The French boys had for some time been going in for gymnastics on homemade bars. They were trying to build up their bicepses to such terrible proportions that the mere sight of their swelling muscles would strike terror into the hearts of their enemies. Whether or not their bicepses were bigger, they seemed to be from the way the French boys swaggered along and from the rumors of the prodigious feats of strength that trickled out of the French section of town.

But all this was nothing to Dusty. "Pooh! They're all muscle-bound," he would say, and he talked so impressively, and took up his complicated stance with such deliberation, and his face wore such a look of serene and indomitable courage, that the French muscle men were impressed in spite of themselves and left him alone. Out in front he would go, drop into position, his chin almost touching the ground, one fist waving back and forth in front of his nose as if brushing away at an imaginary fly and the other pointing at the French like a gun. There he would challenge any one of them to mortal combat, and when nobody accepted, he would straighten up and saunter back with a walk very much like that of a fighting cock. He never kept up his stance very long, however, a fact which didn't surprise Ian after he had secretly tried it a few times; for just to maintain that contortion put such a strain on the backs of his legs that after a minute or two he toppled over exhausted.

But there was another reason why strange gangs hesitated to venture into their territory. This reason was

Oscar. Oscar joined them shortly after Dusty, and immediately became a kind of *de facto* leader. He was the leader because he was so dumb. If he hadn't been so dumb, he would have been in high school playing with boys his own age, but he couldn't ever get out of grade seven, so he played with them, and because he was too big to argue with he was the leader. Nobody minded, because Oscar only got an idea once in a blue moon, although when he did get an idea of something to do he was very stubborn about it and made them all do it no matter how crazy it was. If anyone protested, he just twisted their arm a little, grinning at them. He was slow moving and clumsy, with a scraggle of hairs on his chin and enormous muscles, which he would get them all to feel at least once a day. He was always watching them with a look of sly amusement in his little eyes, as if they were a funny breed of ants that he might decide to step on at any moment. To crown it all he had a lisp.

They formed a gang and called themselves, with fine irony, THE QUAKERS. They were sure everybody would get the point; namely that they were so rough and so tough that this peaceful name would send a special thrill of horror through all who thought of opposing them. The shoe factory was their secret and invincible headquarters. Once they were inside that immense fastness and had pulled the plank over after them, they liked to think that nobody in the world could get at them.

They spent hours in this retreat inventing innumerable rules and rituals. For a few weeks, before the novelty wore off, they had so many rules that merely carrying them out occupied all their time. Guards had to be placed, casual but suspicious-looking passers-by "shadowed," and involved scouting missions into enemy territory carried out. They had a grip and a password; they tampered with the Morse code and mirror writing; and Peebles even claimed to have a formula for invisible ink, the principle ingredient of which was lemon juice. The only trouble was he couldn't remember what it was that made the ink *visible.* Although they tried everything they could think of, from milk to kerosene, it remained invisible forever.

Their enemies multiplied by the hour. They began by fancying that old Cotter, sitting in front of his tinsmith shop, was actually a dope peddler. They played this game so long that unless they thought about it hard they actually believed that he *was* a dope peddler. They kept a spy on him for hours, and they knew that every time he shook hands with a passer-by he was really slipping a small packet of dope to an accomplice. It was no accident that his shop was where Croft and Albion Streets met and that he spent so much time just sitting out front.

Once when Ian was casually loitering by "on duty," old Cotter without warning shot out his long arm and seized him firmly by the coat collar. Then there followed one of the strangest conversations ever to take place on this planet — one that old Cotter remembered for a long time.

"Hold up there a minute, sonny," said old Cotter. "I got a few questions I want to ask you."

Ian stared back at him wildly. He knew he was in a tight spot, and he knew that these dope peddlers were desperate characters. He wondered if he ought to give the emergency signal for help.

"Now then," old Cotter gave his collar a twist, "what in

sam hill are you kids up to, peeking at me all day long from behind the grocery store?"

Ian hesitated for just an instant while two worlds hovered in the balance, the dull real world and the glorious world of make-believe. With an effort he held to the better one. "We're on to you, that's all," he said out of the corner of his mouth.

"Oh ho! *You're* on to *me*, are you." Old Cotter put his head back to take a better look at the situation. "Well, I'm on to you too. I wasn't born yesterday —" He stopped short, as if aware that this was something of an understatement. "You boys are thinking to sneak into my back shop while I'm out here and steal a pair of my best shears. Eh? Isn't that it? I'm not so dumb as I look — eh?" He gave Ian's collar a twist.

"You just better look out, that's all." Ian let a sneer creep into his voice. He had just caught sight of Ely's face peering around the corner of Mooney's junk shop. "You better let go of my collar or you'll get peppered."

"Peppered!" Old Cotter's eyes opened wide. "You feel all right, boy?"

"Sure I feel all right, but I wouldn't be sitting in your shoes."

"You haven't been drinking something you shouldn't, have you, boy?" Old Cotter looked at him closely. "Haven't found an old bottle with some whiskey left in it — nothing like that, eh?"

Ian ignored the insult. "We're about ready to turn you in," he said loudly, more for Ely's benefit than old Cotter's.

"Turn me *in!*" Old Cotter's eyes blurred a little, as if he wasn't sure he was really awake.

"In to the police. That's where." He wondered if he was doing quite the right thing, telling Cotter so much.

"Ha!" said old Cotter. "And that's just where I was thinking of turning you in. Isn't that funny?"

"You haven't got anything on me."

Old Cotter's eye brightened. "Disturbing the peace — *my* peace — that's what I got on you. Now what have you got on me — eh?"

At that moment Ian ducked and was free. "Dope!" he shouted. "That's what we got on you." He tore across the street. But just before he rounded the junk shop, he took one last look back. Old Cotter was sitting motionless staring after him. He certainly looked worried.

"Was that ever a close shave!" he gasped to Ely, who was sitting on an empty orange crate waiting for him.

Ely wasn't impressed. "Captain wants you," he said laconically.

They went down the alley together and across Douglas Avenue to the shoe factory. In the shadow of the factory Ely gave the signal, an imitation of a tomcat in mating season. Looking up, they saw a piece of broken mirror flashing high up in a third-story window. It was the all clear signal, and they climbed at once to the shed roof, where the plank came sliding out of the factory window. Once they were inside, Dusty with a bandanna over his face led them up a flight of stairs, and along a hall until they came to a closed door with a skull drawn in chalk on the panel. Dusty rapped three times, the door opened slowly, and they stepped into a room containing two backless chairs and a desk with three legs. Behind the desk lolled Captain Oscar. He was in the act of peeling the tinsel from a chocolate bar.

"Number two reporting, sir." Dusty pulled the bandanna away from his mouth.

"Thow your badth, number two." The Captain stuffed a piece of chocolate into his mouth.

Ian lifted the lapel of his jacket, revealing a round piece of tin with the number 2 scratched on it. "Old Cotter caught me," he said, "but I got away all right." He spoke with a drawl. He felt quite remarkable. He had been captured and he had escaped.

The Captain munched his chocolate thoughtfully. He looked at Ely, then at Dusty, who was straddling one of the chairs, chewing his nails. Suddenly his dull eye brightened above his bulging cheeks. "You thouldn't of let yourthelf get caught," he said.

"Heck, I didn't know he suspected anything. I was just strolling along, not looking at him or anything, when, bingo, out he reached and grabbed me. I didn't have a chance."

"You thouldn't of pathed tho clothe." The Captain pushed the remains of the chocolate bar into his mouth; his eyes were wet slits.

Ian felt a shiver run along his spine. He didn't like that look in Oscar's eyes. It meant that one of his rare ideas was being born. He suddenly wished that he was safe at home.

The Captain looked at the others. "I gueth he'll have to pay the penalty."

Ian swallowed and stared uneasily out of the window. The room was very still.

"Uh — " The Captain stopped. "Uh — " He started again, stopped and looked up at the ceiling. "I gueth we better hold a meeting to dethide the penalty," he said.

Ely was suddenly all eagerness, as if he had been racking his brains all the time on the problem. "We ought to send a scout over to see what the French gang is up to," he said, and his dark eyes leaped from face to face.

Oscar shut *his* eyes tight. He knew there was some connection, but try as he would he couldn't find it. He opened his eyes and stared hard at Ely. In his preoccupation he swallowed a whole mouthful of chocolate without tasting it, and a quick look of disappointment flickered over his pudding face. They all held their breaths, especially Ian. "Thatth a good idea," he said at last. "Who'll we thend?"

"Ian. Send Ian. That's the penalty," Ely burst out impatiently.

Oscar eyed him, then grinned happily. "There," he said. "Thatth right." He looked at Ian. "Go on over there and thee what they're up to."

A lump came into Ian's throat, and something hard pulled at the corners of his mouth. In a flash every one of those French muscle boys assumed gigantic proportions. He saw himself surrounded, captured, tied, gagged and submitted to unspeakable tortures. He clenched his fists as he mentally punched them into Ely's treacherous little face. "It's too late to go over there before supper," he said desperately.

"Whatth the matter?" said Oscar. "Thcared?"

"Nah — who's scared of them?"

"That's the old spirit." Dusty got up from his chair.

"Just give them the old one-two." He jumped and crouched about the room jabbing fiercely.

"He can go after supper all right," Ely said. "Make him go all the way over to the icehouse and bring back one of those yellow bricks they got piled up there. That'll prove he didn't just hide somewhere and pretend he went."

So it was decided. He walked home alone through the dusty alleys. Even the cats avoided him, and the old dog that hung around B.J.'s shop sniffed once at his feet and slunk off. The late afternoon sun painted the warped clapboards of the livery stable with bronze and rust colors, over the molasses puncheons hung the heady incense of a rich fermentation, and all his wonderful world was an old and wrinkled desert. He didn't even have the zest to climb the fences, and went out past the livery stable to the street.

At supper he had no appetite, and his mother began to worry. "I think he's running around too much," she said. "On the go from dawn to dark with that gang." Her eyes brooded over him.

His father looked at him. "He does look a bit peeked. You better stay in tonight after supper."

He felt a surge of relief. All he had to do was tell them his father wouldn't let him go out after supper. Perhaps by tomorrow they would have forgotten the whole thing.

"I'm just going to take a quiet little walk," he said. "I won't run."

Ely was waiting for him at the corner. "It's a good time to go," he said by way of molification. "They'll all be eating their suppers."

"How'd you like to come along if it's such a good time?" Ian said.

"Sure I'd go along, only I gotta go right back and help my grandfather separate the rotten potatoes from the good ones in the cellar." Ely had a flair for odd excuses.

Ian didn't even bother to comment.

They stopped beside the railroad tracks, while a long freight pulled slowly past. It occurred to Ian that he could oh so easily swing himself up onto one of those iron ladders as they slipped past almost within reach and so be carried out of the town and away so far that he need never come back until he was grown up and famous. Tomorrow's papers would have his picture on the front page, they would call out the fire department and volunteers to look for him, the whistle would blow and his mother would be brokenhearted.

The caboose clattered by, with a trainman standing on the steps swinging his red lantern, and there before them, gray and ominous in the dusk, lay Fuller Street. He moved away from Ely and across the tracks. Away in the distance at the far end of the street loomed the shadow of the icehouse. He walked fast. He didn't even stop at the window of the French pastry shop, the most fascinating window in town. He kept his eyes fixed on the icehouse, and when he was almost there, he couldn't help it, he broke into a run.

At the icehouse he picked up two bricks instead of one. He felt a little safer with a brick in either hand.

Going back was better. It was darker and he was headed for home. He reached the pastry shop. He saw the red and green blinkers of the railroad tracks. He was almost safe. He decided to make a dash for it, and then without warning, the whole French gang slipped quietly out from behind the pastry shop and quickly formed a circle about him. Ian's heart sank. He fixed his eyes on the thin face of their leader, Pee Wee LeBlanc, and he was all at once so scared that his legs fairly wobbled.

"Well, well, if it isn't one a dose Crescent Street sissies," Pee Wee said. "What you doin over here on dis side a town, sissy face?"

His mouth felt like a stretched rubber band. "Just minding my own business," he managed to say. He didn't want to answer so boldly, but the words came out willy-nilly.

"Oh. Da Crescent Street sissy wants to be sassy?" Pee Wee's voice went hard. He looked around. "What'll we do wid dis spy?"

"Tie him up and drop in da crick," came a high pitched voice.

"Dig a hole down behind Gagnon's barn and bury him alive up to his neck and let da rats chew off his ears," came another squeeky voice.

"Na! Tie him to da tracks and let da Ocean Limited run over him."

They crowded in closer. He kept turning around. "Listen," he said, "the first guy that touches me I'll conk him with one of these bricks."

"Oh ho," said Pee Wee slyly. "Look, da sissy face's got a couple of bricks. He's been stealin bricks." He was silent for a moment, studying the situation. "All right," he said, "we'll give you a fair chance to show weder ya got any guts." He pushed forward the smallest boy in the circle, a little fellow barely up to Ian's shoulder. He stood there spitting sideways, hitching up his belt and eying Ian fiercely out of big black eyes. His nose was running in a little dribble down his upper lip, and every once in a while he sniffed hard and the dribble went back up his nose.

"Put dem bricks down," Pee Wee said silkily, "and if ya can beat dis wee little guy fair, we'll let ya go."

"Yeah!" said the little fellow, puffing out his chest like a bird taking a bath. "Come on and fight." He held up his fists and danced around the circle.

Ian watched him as if he were a little wasp, and shame and fear welled up inside his chest. The strange surroundings, the hostile circle, his loneliness, the darkness, all sapped his courage like a poison. His heart pounded. He didn't want to fight anybody. He backed away from the little fellow, thinking only of some way to escape, and when somebody pushed the little fellow on top of him he jumped back like a timid rabbit.

"Come on," they called. "Chicken liver!" They reveled in their disgust, laughing and slapping each other on the back at such a spectacle.

He glanced at the lighted window of the pastry shop, wondering if there was any use in calling for help, and all at once he had an idea, an idea born of desperation. Without another thought, he drew back his arm, and while all the boys on that side ducked, he threw one of the bricks straight at the window in the door of the pastry shop. There was a loud crash and a cry of rage from inside as the brick plunked into a large cake on a shelf beside the door. For a moment the entire circle of French boys just stared at the broken window with their mouths open, and then like magic they vanished, vanished as if the ground had swallowed them up, and the next instant Ian was tearing wildly along the street toward those green and red blinkers.

And as he ran through the darkness all he could think of was what a coward he had been — what a miserable, yellow, chickenhearted, lily-livered coward — to back away from that little fellow with the runny nose. He came up over the tracks and in his hurry slipped, ripping his trouser leg and cutting his knee. On the other side of the tracks in the shadow of the shoe factory he stopped and looked up at the rows of windows gleaming faintly. Suddenly on an impulse he threw the remaining brick up at those windows. In a moment there came back to him a small crash and the tinkle of broken glass.

So he had done it — had thrown a brick at Uncle Rufus' factory — broken one more window. The shock of realization of what he had done sobered him and he went slowly on around the factory and home.

He tried to slip upstairs without being noticed, but his mother came out into the hall. Her eye ran over him from his wet, matted hair and flushed cheeks to the rip in his trousers.

"A nice, quiet little walk," she said, and her voice sounded flat and tired. She moved up the stairs behind him. "Sometimes I almost wish you were a girl," she said.

He was quiet, thinking how simple life must be for a girl.

The odd thing was that the boys never asked him for the brick, never even asked him if he had gone over to Fuller Street at all. Captain Oscar did look at him once through the day as if he had something on his mind but nothing ever came of it.

It was getting colder. The green mantle of leaves that concealed the town's dinginess was gone, and the houses lay gray and bare under the open sky. It was clear how many of them needed painting. "A hard winter coming," the old men prophesied, and his father complained of the price of coal. The men standing on the corners in their old mackinaws and sweaters had a bleak and strained look. Old Mr. Ferray went around trying to sell cucumbers for pickling, but nobody seemed to have any money. The young men all went down to the marshes to catch muskrat. "They'll glut the market as sure as day," his father predicted. His mother let out Ian's winter coat once more. "That's the end of the seam," she said. And Uncle Rufus came down in the morning stretching and swinging his arms. "Here I am," he would say, "in the prime of life — and nothing for me to do — nothing. Is that right, I ask you?" he would glare at them.

"Now, now," Ian's mother would say, "you've earned yourself a good rest."

"Rest!" The word infuriated him. "I don't want to rest the rest of my life though!" He would pour his two heaping teaspoons of sugar into his tea and stir it so that it slopped into the saucer. "Full of energy and no initiative — no more initiative than a snail."

"If you would just forget about the factory and look around, you might find something to interest you," Ian's mother said.

"Pah!" said his father.

But the QUAKERS were working on a new project — a gymnasium — a gymnasium that would give them such muscles that they would bust all the seams of all their clothes and scare the living daylights out of the French boys at the mere sight of them.

They hardly had time to eat they were so busy. They had cleared out a room high up on the top floor in the exact center of the shoe factory under a great square sky-light, and here they labored day after day. Loafing men on the corners would stare at them oddly as they dashed by with a wild light in their eyes and some mystifiying piece of equipment over their shoulders that they had salvaged from some forgotten rubbish heap or old Mooney's junk yard.

For days they scrubbed and swept, pounded nails, and sawed boards. They made a muscle builder that should have been listed among the wonders of the modern world, an incredible maze of rubber strips cut from old inner tubes. Once you were encased in this contraption, you had to develop your muscles, and your intelligence too, to escape its crushing embrace. They had skipping ropes and acrobatic bars, and from a beam overhead a knotted rope up which you could pull yourself hand over hand. They lugged immense quantities of iron at night from the junk yard to make weights, iron rods with bunches of clanking iron tied to each end with chain. To lift one of these weights from the floor two inches taxed their utmost strength. Even Oscar could barely lift them to his knees. Under Dusty's guidance they even tried to construct a treadmill from a large barrel that turned on a greased pole, but this proved better adapted to developing a sense of balance than anything else, for nobody ever managed to stay on it long enough to take more than three or four strides.

In the center they roped off a boxing ring, carefully measured to regulation size, but in order to enclose it in taut ropes, a complicated web of old clotheslines was strung in every direction throughout the room. You never dared move quickly or carelessly about the gymnasium, for if you weren't tripped by one rope, you were likely to be garroted by another. When all the contraptions were in use, a clamor filled the placed that would have put a boiler factory to shame. At such times people passing along Douglas Avenue would stop and listen and stare up at the shoe factory with a puzzled look, and once a rumor started that the factory was running again, but it soon died. The noise that started the rumor was Dusty punching the ancient punching bag he had resurrected from some secret source along with the ratty boxing gloves. They were all training hard to be boxing champions. Oscar was going to be a heavyweight. "Feel thothe muthleth," he would demand every five minutes. "Jutht wait till Dempthey feelth them." He would go off chuckling and nodding his head with mirth at what a surprise was in store for Dempsey. "I jutht hope he lathth till I get there," he would say. Dusty was eating like mad to build himself up for the light heavyweight class. If he got to be a light heavyweight he was going to challenge all the heavyweights anyway. And every night before retiring Ian carefully measured his upper arm to see how much his muscle had grown. But it was discouraging how slowly it grew, how many hours of sweating exercise showed no results whatever.

Only on Sunday did they stay away from the place, impatient and bored. Sunday, the day of rest, was something of an anomaly in a town where most of the men had already rested the other six days. Still, it was kept rigidly. On Sunday the town grew so dead you could hear the people breathing. If a cat meowed or sneezed even, the sound was very clear and lonely.

On Sunday morning Ian would come out to the back-door steps with his father, and they would polish their shoes together, the flat can of shoe polish between them, his father standing with one foot on the upper step, while Ian sat on the lower one and rubbed the polish on with a rag. Mr. Antonelli would usually come by in his white shoes and hat with his four daughters walking sedately behind him in silk dresses puffing out under their dark blue reefers. They would be coming from Mass. Francesca would smile at him slyly around her father's shoulder, her eyes dark and shining under her amazingly thick lashes.

He never knew what to say to her.

When his father had finished, he straightened up, put his thumbs under his suspenders, and if the weather was mild walked slowly up the length of the yard and back again. It was his sole recreation on the Sabbath. Ian stayed sprawled out on the steps. Sometimes a fly buzzed about his head, or a toilet flushed somewhere, and then nearly always, old Mrs. Gallup began playing "Rock of Ages" on her piano.

His father would come slowly back down the yard, stop in front of him and say, "It's time to tidy up for church."

Then Peebles might come around the corner in a suit.

If he did, they would look at each other with lackluster eyes, and Peebles would say, "Goin to church?" and when Ian nodded, he would add, "Well, see you in Sunday school."

On the way to church he would trail a little behind his father. The air would be full of the ringing of bells. He could pick them out. The great booming one, the Catholic bell, with the Anglican ringing in little quick strokes in between. But somewhere off in the distance was another bell, ringing so faintly that he wasn't sure it was there at all, but when the Catholic bell stopped, and then the Anglican stopped as if just waiting for the Catholic to stop first, then the other bell kept on ringing, and as it rang, by a kind of magic Ian could see all the houses and streets of the town spread out under the blue sky, and the whole town was beautiful and mournful and fading away under the sound of that distant bell.

Up and down the street he could see the old people, singly and in couples, walking to church. For Sunday was the day all the old people came out from wherever they stayed the rest of the week. The old people liked Sunday, especially the old women, who gathered around the church door after the sermon was over, bobbing their heads, shaking hands endlessly, as if the most wonderful thing in the world was that they were there again and had lived another week. They tottered and fluttered and leaned toward each other in an ecstasy of congratulation, and they whispered endlessly as if everything were a secret.

He followed his father past the blank green windows of the closed stores until they came to Victoria Street and the public square where the same old loafers sat on the benches along with one or two strange tramps who were spending Sunday in town. Down Victoria Street they went, past Watling's Ladies' Wear, and Moffat's Grocery, and there was the church in all its magnificence on the corner — the Presbyterian Church!

What a beautiful building! All yellow brick and red brick and cobblestones set in cement, and stucco full of bits of purple glass, with a green copper roof and a steeple. There was a clock on the steeple, but it didn't tell time any more, and there was no bell. His father said the Presbyterians let the other churches ring the bells, and that it was very clever because it saved a lot of money. But there were stained glass windows of the Good Samaritan, of Moses and the Rock, with the white water gushing forth, and of Jesus healing the sick. When you were inside on a Sunday morning those windows glowed like colored fire, and you couldn't take your eyes off them. Mr. Rustrum the minister didn't seem half so real waving his arms behind the pulpit in his black gown. Whenever Mr. Rustrum stood up, Ian immediately went into a kind of trance from which he did not emerge until the organ, leaping into high and cheerful music, signaled that the sermon was over. Then the congregation rose with a sigh and a rustle, and there began the interminable, slow movement along the aisles. Like thick honey the people flowed toward the vestibule, slowed almost to a stop by the old ladies leaning over to clutch a neighbor by the arm, their long white gloves fluttering, their voices whispering hollowly under the dome of the church. And like a fly stuck in the middle, holding his breath so he wouldn't have to smell the sticky perfume, Ian shrank to lonely insignificance.

On such a Sunday toward the very end of October, Ian and Peebles made their way slowly to afternoon Sunday school. The street was so dull that although they counted all the telephone poles and leaped over all the hydrants and examined all the empty cigarette packages lying in the gutter because Peebles had once found an unused cigarette in one, they reached Victoria Square in no time at all. As he always did, Peebles insisted that they walk around in the grass looking for the nickels and dimes that must have been lost by the Saturday night crowd listening to the band concert. They never found anything, and Peebles was always planning to get up early some Sunday morning and come up to the square before the tramps picked up the money.

As they turned to leave, an old hobo in a battered hat and several days' beard suddenly hailed them from one of the benches. "Hello, buddies," he said, "where are you off to all dressed up?"

They turned sharply and looked at him. His face was almost black with train soot from riding the rails, but wrinkled like an old shoe when he grinned. His brown eyes twinkled with good will.

"Sunday school," Ian said.

"Ah that's good. That's fine." The old tramp reached over and touched him lightly on the arm. "I allus went to Sunday school when I was your age." His brown eyes narrowed. "Now I'm a lost sinner, headed right for —" He hiccuped a breath of whiskey fumes into their faces — "the bad place."

They stared at him, fascinated to be so close to one doomed to that place.

He leaned forward, his voice dropping a whole octave as he took them into his confidence. "You boys got yer collection money all safe and sound in yer pockets?"

They glanced at each other.

"Better feel and make sure. Pockets sometimes has holes, and a nickel or a dime can roll out of a mighty small hole." He stopped short. "What does yer pops give ya fer collection — a nickel or a dime?"

"Just a nickel." Peebles felt in his pocket.

"Well that aint enough fer big boys like you. You tell yer pops you want to give more next Sunday." He broke into a phlegmy cough and spat over the back of the bench.

They waited patiently for him to go on. He made them feel important.

He turned back to them, his eyes all watery from coughing. He slapped his chest. "No lungs left. Air just goes in and out." He gave them a crinkled smile. "Now what do you suppose they does with all that money they collects from Sunday school?"

"Why uh — they pay the minister," said Peebles.

"And the organ player, Mrs. Frazee," said Ian.

"Poh!" broke in the tramp. "Why that don't amount to nothing outa all those collections. What does they do, now, with the rest of it?" He leaned forward, watching them intently.

"Uh — they give it to the poor," said Ian.

The tramp slapped his hand down hard on his knee. "That's right," he said, "that's exactly right. Now —" He scratched one side of his beard quickly and hunched forward on the bench. "Now do you boys happen to know who is the poorest, most unfortunate, forsaken individual in this town right this minute — the most in need of a bit of Christian charity?"

They waited.

"Me," he said and leaned back triumphantly, pulling inside out, as he did so, both pants pockets. "I aint got a solitary nickel. Not a penny to buy a bite of supper with. Why —" he hiccuped — "you boys are practically millionaires alongside of me — with yer nice nickels in yer pockets that yer all set to give away to the poor — practically millionaires."

They looked at him with condescending pity.

"The trouble is, that by the time they get all that money counted out and sorted and divided up, it'll be too late to do me any good. I'll be dead and in my grave of starvation." He waved a hand. "Of course some poor devil just like me will get it — but not me — not me. And the preacher'll get all the credit for helpin *that* poor fellow.

Not you boys — oh no — not you who really gave the money. But as fer me —"

"Here," said Ian, and he reached out and dropped his nickel into the tramp's ready palm. "I might as well give it to you direct."

"Me too," said Peebles as he handed over his nickel.

The old tramp's face fell open like a split watermelon, showing his two big yellow teeth — the only upper teeth he had. "Yer a couple of gentlemen," he said, "a couple of real Christians. Now you run along to Sunday school and when the plate comes along, you put yer hand over it quick and tap it with yer fingernail. That's what I used to do."

They were silent as they walked away. Ian could feel his charity like a mantle of gold over his shoulders.

"That was a pretty nice old tramp," Peebles said.

"If you ask me, *he* was a true Christian gentleman," said Ian firmly.

Sunday school met in an assembly room separated from the main auditorium of the church by a most remarkable wall that was divided right down the middle and could be mysteriously rolled apart for special services. As they entered the room, Mr. Diblee, the Sunday school superintendent, was already waving his hand back and forth, and everybody was singing "Brighten the Corner Where You Are." They slipped into the last row and joined in loudly, trying to make their voices stand out above all the others. Mrs. Diblee at the piano jerked up her head at the raucous new note, and a pained expression spread across her features, while all the sweet little-girl voices seemed to falter, like a flock of birds that had suddenly lost their way.

After the singing Mr. Diblee told them a story about a very honest little boy who had found a purse full of money and had returned it to a rich old lady who adopted him and brought him up in her big house and sent him away to college, where he studied hard and later became even richer than the old lady. Then they sang "Jesus Bids Us Shine," and after that they read a psalm. Mr. Diblee read one line and they roared the other back at him. It was great fun.

In the midst of the reading, Peebles leaned forward and whispered hoarsely that old Mr. Delahunt wasn't there. Immediately they grew tense. Mr. Delahunt taught them their lesson in one of the little cubicles that lined the Sunday school room. He was about sixty-five years old and unbelievably patient. There was simply nothing they could do to make him excited or cross. As a result their weekly lesson was beyond doubt the craziest lesson in the world. While Mr. Delahunt read the lesson, they sat on the bench that ran round the wall of the tiny cubicle and talked away as if Mr. Delahunt didn't exist. They threw spitballs at each other, occasionally hitting Mr. Delahunt's bald head, tried to push each other off the bench, played tag, and raised such a racket that the teacher in the next cubicle would begin banging on the wall. But Mr. Delahunt just set in the middle of the bedlam and read serenely on, never looking up from the book. And when it came time for the questions, he would ask them and answer them.

But today Mr. Delahunt was missing. The wonderful news spread rapidly among the members of his class. It had happened once or twice before and nobody but they had missed him. So when it came time for the lessons, they marched dutifully off to their cubicle, and as soon as the assembly room was empty, they crept out again one by one like a band of thieves.

The whole church lay before them deserted and undefended, like a city to be sacked — an immense place of endless passageways and secret doors to sanctorums never entered, except perhaps by Mr. Rustrum himself. Ian and Peebles separated from the others. First they ran up the stairs to the choir room. They opened a door in the wall and found themselves standing before the elaborate array of ropes and pulleys that moved the big partition. They glanced at each other with bright eyes and with one accord took hold of the nearest rope and began to pull. There came a low rumbling that shook the floor slightly beneath them. They heaved again and again until the rope wouldn't move any more. Then they ran back to the assembly room to see the effect, and there before their delighted eyes was a great ten-foot gap in the wall through which they could see the shadowy depths of the main auditorium. They bent double with silent mirth. What a surprise for Mr. Diblee.

But they had no time to waste. They hurried back through the choir room and down a winding staircase. On a landing they found a very tiny door opening on a low dark passageway. As Ian followed Peebles along this tunnel, little shivers ran along his spine. Everything about the church was mysterious. The ultimate mysteries of life might be found in such dark places — some great book with all the answers. He would hardly have been surprised if he had come upon God himself with a long beard presiding over a committee of angels at the end of this passageway. Instead they found themselves in a place so fantastic that for a moment they just stood holding their breath. What kind of an infernal machine was it, with great pipes twisting like snakes and levers and wires? Then it dawned on them. They were inside the pipe organ. "Gee!" exclaimed Peebles, and his voice went whistling and fluting up through the pipes until it seemed that a hundred boys were up there, all saying "Gee!" in every note of the scale. They tiptoed forward.

"Look!" Ian pointed toward the big bellows. He pulled a lever, and an eerie rush of wind filled their ears. He pulled another lever, and immediately, like the roar of an angry lion, a terrific blast of sound rolled and thundered about them. They clapped their hands to their ears; they were drowning in sound. Ducking their heads, they dashed back along the passageway. Once Ian's foot caught in a wire, and it snapped with an angry twang, but they didn't stop until they were back in the choir room. They stood panting and listening, sure that everyone in the church must have heard that mighty blast of sound, but all that came to their ears was the soft drone of voices reciting in the cubicles.

They walked out onto the platform of the big auditorium. Ian stood behind the pulpit and waved his arms madly and made terrible faces at an imaginary audience. Then they ran down the steps, up the aisles and up another flight of steps to the balcony. From the balcony they caught a glimpse away across the church of two other wayward boys peering at them with astonishment and half-frightened eyes through the great gap in the wall. They almost choked with laughter.

"I bet they think the church is haunted," Peebles said gleefully.

At the rear of the balcony was a door that was always locked, but now Peebles got out his master skeleton key, guaranteed to open any lock, and in no time they were running up a narrow winding stairway. Dazzled by their own daring, they realized that they were in the very steeple of the church. At the top of the stairway was a tiny room full of machinery. They were, in fact, right behind the big face of the clock. To their surprise it wasn't an imitation clock after all, but a real clock, an enormous clock, with cogwheels almost as large as bicycle wheels, and a curved bell with a clapper for striking the hours.

"This old clock is slow," Peebles said, pulling out his Ingersoll. His watch said five minutes to three, while the hands of the clock in the steeple had been at twenty minutes past one as long as they could remember. So they turned the hands and set it right.

"I wonder why they don't get this old clock fixed," Ian said.

"The Presbyterians are too stingy to fix it," Peebles said.

"Yeah, I guess they are," Ian said. "Anyway it's time to get back to the Sunday school room. Mr. Diblee will be coming out."

They moved around the works of the clock.

"You'd think they'd get a new clock," Ian said disgustedly and gave the nearest cogwheel a hard kick. Then he jumped back aghast, the hair fairly rising on the top of his head, for the old clock gave a sort of groan, then a wheeze, and then, with every little cogwheel creaking, they all started turning merrily, and a loud "tick-tock, tick-tock" like the sound of someone tapping a table with a spoon sounded through the little room.

All the way down the narrow spiral staircase they could hear it. Never, never before had they felt quite so close to being gods. Peebles locked the door carefully behind them, and they hurried down to the assembly room. The other boys from their errant class were already in the cubicle when they arrived, all jabbering at once about the strange things that had happened.

"Those were all signs to us for being so bad to old Delahunt," Peebles said solemnly. He and Ian were actually hardly listening to the others at all. They were listening with their heads cocked to see what would happen at three o'clock. Seeing them, the others began to listen too.

"I think there will be another sign at exactly three o'clock," Ian said.

"Aye — a sign from above." Peebles frowned and took out his Ingersoll. "It's almost three now."

The others shuffled uneasily, staring at the watch.

Then it happened. "Bonggg! Bonggg! Bonggg!" One of the boys jumped straight up, his hair rising.

A gentle sigh escaped simultaneously from Ian and Peebles, and they sank back against the wall smiling.

The next instant Mr. Diblee's shrill whistle sounded, and they all rushed out into the Sunday school assembly room. Mr. Diblee and a little group of teachers were standing together looking at the opening in the wall.

After a few seconds one of the teachers went up into the choir room and tried to put the wall together again, but nothing happened. Mr. Diblee stood up on the platform and stared down at them sternly. "Does anyone know anything about this?" he asked.

Nobody answered.

"Well —" Mr. Diblee looked at the opening and gave his head a shake. "Well —" He raised his hand. "Let us all sing 'Dare to be a Daniel!' " he ended lamely. Mrs. Diblee banged the piano, and everybody began to sing.

But no one sang with the enthusiasm of Ian and Peebles. "Dare to be a Daniel!" they roared. "Dare to stand alone! Dare to have a purpose firr — um, dare to make it known!" And such was the volume of sound they generated that even Mr. Diblee glanced in their direction once or twice and almost stopped waving his hand back and forth.

For the rest of the afternoon Ian sat curled up in the corner chair in the parlor reading *The Mysterious Island* by Jules Verne — all about a group of men who landed on a desert island with nothing but a watch and ended up with a mountain stronghold with elevators, running water and pet monkeys. What a glorious adventure! he thought over and over. Oh to be wrecked on a South Sea island! His mother had to call him three times for supper.

After supper his mother and father went to church, and he went back to his adventures in the South Seas. He was busily engaged in capturing a wild monkey with a liana net when he heard his mother's voice at the front door. She was talking quite loud and quite fast. "Everybody in town is talking about it," she was saying. "That clock hasn't been going for twenty years." The door opened and she came into the parlor with old Mrs. Gallup hanging on her arm.

"*Twenty* years!" exclaimed old Mrs. Gallup. "More like thirty!"

"And that isn't all by any means," his mother went on, hardly able to control her voice. "When Mrs. Frazee went to play the organ, not a thing happened. The janitor pumped and pumped, but not a solitary note came out." She paused to catch her breath. "I wish you could have seen the look on Mrs. Frazee's face. She had to go play the old piano down below the pulpit. And there was that big gap in the assembly wall. Mr. Rustrum hinted *very* strongly —" her voice dropped, "that the Catholics are involved. 'It could be the religious wars starting,' he said." She stared for several seconds at Mrs. Gallup. "It really *was* spooky. You'd almost think it was a sign or something."

"The ways of the Almighty are strange," said old Mrs. Gallup piously. "Perhaps it is a sign that the Lord hasn't forgotten this town altogether."

Ian got up quietly. He felt that he was about to burst.

"Where are *you* going?" his mother asked.

"To get a drink of water." His voice seemed to him all muffled up in his throat.

"Oh?" She looked at him strangely — a half-puzzled expression suddenly coming into her face, a startled look, as if she had started off for somewhere and had suddenly remembered that she had forgotten something, but couldn't remember what. It made her look like a young girl again. "I was talking to Mrs. Delahunt," she went on slowly, one eye following him to the door — he could feel it. "She said that Mr. Delahunt was quite ill — couldn't teach his class this afternoon." She paused — "Who *did* teach you your Sunday school lesson this afternoon, Ian?" she called.

He stopped. He could feel the hot blood rushing to his cheeks. "Nobody," he said. He went out into the hall.

"It may be that the millennium is coming," he heard old Mrs. Gallup say. "No," his mother said, "I don't think God had anything to do with it after all. When something completely and utterly impossible happens, I know now who's probably had a finger in it — even if I don't clearly see how."

"You mean the devil," said Mrs. Gallup.

"Oh no," said his mother. "Good heavens no." She laughed softly. "Oh, I can still see that Mrs. Frazee's face," she said.

Ian walked softly out to the kitchen.

3

He had a funny sort of adventure in school. There was a new teacher of Latin, a Miss Webb. She was young and very pretty, a fact which made all the boys want to be bad. Ian had captured the seat in the back with the loose nail that screeched when you tipped, but the very first time he tipped, up to the front she brought him and made him sit among the girls, where he felt very uncomfortable with everybody staring at the back of his neck.

"Now I'm not going to keep you very long this morning," Miss Webb said, "but I *do* want to give you a little taste of this delightful language spoken by the Roman conquerors over two thousand years ago. We shall begin with this word." She turned and wrote on the board with large, flowing strokes: AMO. "Now," she said, facing them, "Does anyone know what that word means?" She paused and waited, and after a moment pointed — he thought directly at him. He got very red; he had no idea in the world what the word meant; all he could think of was Bon Ami, the window cleaner his mother used. "Uh —" he said.

There was a slight sound behind him. "To love," a strange voice said, a voice as low and soft as the purr of a kitten. It seemed to go right through him.

"Why, that is correct," said Miss Webb. "I love." She turned to the board, and as if she were playing some kind of game with the word, wrote AMO, AMAS, AMAT, AMAMUS, AMATIS, AMANT. She faced them again. "And can you tell us what these mean?" She smiled at the girl behind Ian.

Again the soft voice brushed against his soul. "I love, you love, he loves. We love, you love, they love."

"Excellent!" cried Miss Webb. "And what is your name?"

"Adrienne."

"You must be a new girl to our school." Miss Webb turned to the class. "This is Adrienne," she said, "who knows how to conjugate the verb to love."

He sat still as a stone, oblivious to the room, Miss Webb, to everything but that new sound. Around and around in a tangled blur of feeling went the new girl's voice, like some soft thing feeling its way, probing, probing, to touch parts of him that had never been touched before. Adrienne — Adrienne — I love, you love, he loves — petals falling on water, spinning and whirling away. How did he know without turning around that she was prettier than any other girl in the class?

Suddenly he heard his name.

"Ian McAleenan, can you tell me what this word means?" Miss Webb's ruler hovered over the board.

"I love," he began.

The class roared at him. They rocked in their seats. He flushed right down to his hands.

Miss Webb regarded him intently, her large, luminous eyes still on his face. He waited for the lash of her sharp tongue. To his surprise her voice was gentle. "No," she said, "you are looking at the wrong verb. This one here is NECO — I kill."

After a while she let them go.

Peebles and Ian walked together along the street. The sun was high. The air was cool, with a smell like cinnamon and apples. "Did you ever hear such dull stuff?" Peebles' voice was laden with disgust. "Amo — amas — amat. What do we have to learn such stuff for? And that girl — that Adrienne — what a teacher's pet."

"Yeah," said Ian, "what a teacher's pet."

Peebles glanced over his shoulder. "She's coming along behind us," he said.

Ian stole a look. She was sauntering along half a block behind them — all alone, swinging her books carelessly at the end of a short strap. She was wearing a plaid coat and her pale oval face, with wide, dark eyes, turned away as he looked at her.

"She's old Dock Bliss's niece. She's staying with them to go to school this winter." Peebles kicked an apple core out of his path. "Aye-dree-en! What a name!"

The next day in school he felt more uncomfortable

than ever up there in the front seat. All he could see from where he sat was Miss Webb's shapely big legs through the the bottom of the desk, crossing and uncrossing, the silk of her stockings whispering. Once when he was staring at them, he looked up and found her eyes resting on his quietly. He blushed violently and looked down at the open book on his desk, pretending to read. He decided that he disliked Miss Webb.

Once during the morning he felt a hand at his shoulder. At first he ignored it, his heart pounding, but when it persisted, he turned around and found himself staring into the new girl's eyes. A little shock ran through his body. He had never seen that kind of look in any eyes before; for a long moment she didn't say anything, just looked at him, and all at once he was tumbling silently through bottomless space. He stared into those limpid eyes until he could see the little green and amber spokes radiating from the black pools in the center. He fought against the clinging, speaking softness that held him like a fly in a web. The silence grew. Then the thick lashes came down like a sleeping doll's. "Could I borrow your eraser?" she said.

He stuck the eraser into her hand and turned back quickly. There was a half-finished algebra problem on the page in front of him. He picked up his pencil, holding it motionless over the paper, but he didn't even see the figures on the page any more. His mind was all turned inward, trying to hold back time, trying with every nerve to hold the image of those lovely eyes, and that strange sweetness running like a comb through his body. He sat rigid, conscious of her just behind him, her hands almost touching him on her desk. He began to will her to touch him, and all at once she did. The blood came rushing to his cheeks. He turned around, his eyes leaping to hers, and again that soft, paralyzing look held him helpless.

"Thanks for your eraser," she whispered.

He looked down at the little hand holding out the eraser. He tried to say something, but he only choked. He wanted to tell her to keep the eraser, but he couldn't say the words. He took it silently, and as he took it somehow her fingers brushed against his. The rest of the morning the main problem in his life was trying to decide whether she had touched his hand on purpose or accidentally.

They were doing something to him — Miss Webb and Adrienne, especially Adrienne. He was like a boy divided in half. He would go up into the gymnasium and slam into the old punching bag until even Dusty stared at him admiringly, yet all the time he would be thinking only of those big dark eyes with the flecks of gold and green. What made him most angry with himself was the horrible conviction that if he lived to be a hundred he would never have the nerve to actually speak to her.

The strain was so great that he took to escaping into a dream world. At night he would lie in bed staring into the darkness and re-create the world closer to his heart's desire. There in the darkness, his eyes wide open, he lived endless adventures with her. There she would walk up to him smiling, or rather ride up on her bicycle — they both had new bicycles in his dream world — and there he had no trouble at all speaking to her. He would smile at her easily, even a little condescendingly, their eyes meeting and holding in long, rapturous glances until she would bend her head, blushing and slowly drawing her eyes away.

"Where shall we go today, Adrienne?" he would say.

"Oh I don't care," she would answer in her whispering husky voice. "It doesn't matter as long as we're together."

"Some of the boys want me to go fishing," he would say.

"Oh!" Her face would register her keen disappointment. "Couldn't we slip away — just *us?*" Her enormous dark eyes would look pleadingly into his.

"Why not?" He would smile down into her face, and they would jump on their new bicycles and go side by side down Church Street, and just as they came to the corner of Spring Street, there would always be Miss Webb coming home from school with an armful of papers, looking at them with astonished eyes. They would go right up over Sand Hill, and sometimes two or three big colored boys would start getting fresh, and one unlucky fellow would say something real sassy. Then he would get off, lay his own bicycle down carefully on the ground, carefully remove his jacket, flip up his shirt cuffs, walk over to the big fellow, and without a word hit him once with a right to the jaw, knocking him out cold. Afterwards Adrienne would look at him with tears of admiration in her eyes, but he would just laugh it off and throw a stern look at the other two colored fellow backing away in dismay.

When they got to the woods, they would hide their new bicycles in a thick grove of spruce trees, and walk hand in hand deeper and deeper into the woods, until they came at last to the bank of a stream. Then she would sit down on the bank and say, "Let's not fish yet for a while, Ian."

And he would stand looking down at her and say, "All right. I guess the fish can wait. What shall we do?" At this point his heart would begin to beat very fast.

She would lean back on one arm and look up at him, her eyes very big and round. "Oh I don't know."

And he would drop down beside her and take her — oh so tenderly — into his arms, looking deep into her eyes, and they would kiss, and kiss and kiss —

That was the way he would make the world over.

But sometimes he was grown up. He had been away and made a fortune, and had come back to town in a big gray Franklin roadster with wire wheels and a musical horn. She would be tall then, just about as tall as Miss Webb. She would be walking down Main Street, and he would roll up to the curb beside her and say, "Hello, Adrienne." Just like that he would say it.

She would turn in surprise, a little frown on her face for the unknown masher, and then she would recognize him and her face would break into a wonderful, dazzling, happy smile. "Why hello, Ian McAleenan." And her face would turn as red as a rose, giving her feelings away completely.

"Hop in," he would say, swinging open the door. "I'll take you for a spin."

They would drive around town for a while, and every so often someone would call out his name from the sidewalk, and he would have to swerve over to the curb. Then good old Peebles would come along. "Holy mackerel!" he would exclaim, "if it isn't that old Quaker, Ian McAleenan!" and he would thrust out his hand and give him the old secret grip. "What have you done, discovered a gold mine or something?"

"Oh no," he would smile quietly, "just a few investments at the right time."

Peebles would lean back then and look at the Franklin. "Some boat," he would say. "How many cylinders?"

"Oh about sixteen," he would answer. "Somewhere around there."

"I'll bet *that* cost you plenty," Peebles would say.

"Just four or five thousand," he would toss off, "chicken feed."

At that moment Miss Webb would come by. At first she wouldn't recognize him, but when she had passed she would turn sharply and come back. "Why if it isn't Ian McAleenan!" she would say in utter surprise.

"Hello Webb," he would say and would generously give her his hand, the one that wasn't holding the cigar. "How's the old school these days — pretty dull, I bet." He would give a chuckle.

"I guess it is a little dull now," she would say and would look at him hard. "I hear you've made a fortune."

"Oh a few million." He would flick his ash over the side of the car. "Wasn't hard except for the first million. I was figuring out how to do it back in school when the other kids were studying Latin — "

Miss Webb's face would get a little red at that, but she'd take it like a good sport. "I guess some just don't need an education," she'd say. "They're just naturally brilliant." She would smile and say goodbye, nodding to Peebles and Adrienne.

"Say," he would call after her. "I'd like to give the kids at the old school a break. How about giving them the afternoon off for a picnic in Hickey's Grove? Everything at my expense — pop, ice cream, chocolates, prizes — How about it?"

"Wonderful. That's a wonderful idea, Ian!" she would call back. "We'll do it this very afternoon."

Then he'd start up the motor, say goodbye to Peebles, and he and Adrienne would shoot right out of town in the big Franklin along the paved highway over the marshes. He'd let her out to about ninety, and Adrienne would sort of snuggle up beside him holding his arm tight. "Don't be frightened," he would say, "I can handle this old crate."

They'd stop off over in Springdale, where he would buy a couple of double-scoop chocolate sodas, and they would talk seriously for a while, sipping their sodas.

"I suppose you're married by now," he would say, letting a little note of sadness come into his voice.

She would look away, embarrassed, and almost whisper, "No, I'm not, Ian."

"What!" he would exclaim. "Not married! The prettiest girl in town?"

"I just wasn't interested in — in any of the boys left around town," she would answer.

They would be silent after that for a while, and then he would say it — just as easily as cutting cheese — "You know I always loved you, Adrienne."

Her big eyes would come up slowly to his. Slowly her cheeks would flush scarlet. She would bite her lips a little to keep them from trembling.

"But of course you never cared," he would add.

"Oh, but I did!" The words would burst from her with a little sob, and she would put her hand on his arm. "I always loved you. I never loved anyone else. I think I fell in love with you that first day I saw you in eight B — *Amo, amas, amat* — remember?"

"No, I don't remember that," he would say, "but I remember how I loved you."

They would look at each other for a long time then. Her face would be bright and glowing.

"Will you marry me, Adrienne?" he would say quietly.

"Yes, Ian." Her thick lashes would lie along her cheeks and her voice would be so low that he would have to lean forward. And she would lift up her mouth, and they would kiss and kiss.

But the next day at school he wouldn't speak to her all day long. He would just sit in front of her, not even seeing her except when she went to the board or for the brief moment when he came toward her to take his seat. All morning long and all afternoon he would sit there in front of her thinking of nothing else and not once seeing her. Afraid to turn around. Almost feeling her breath sometimes on the back of his neck, and sometimes her hand as it accidentally touched the collar of his jacket. But never turning around — afraid of paradise as if it were full of scorpions. He thought he would go mad.

He was saved by ice. Nature saved him. The day that

glorious shout was raised on the play field by the school: "There's ice on Christie's Pond. They're skating on Christie's Pond" — on that day he became at once half free again.

When he and Peebles rushed down to the pond behind the coffin factory, a marvelous scene was spread out before their eyes. There was the pond, smooth and black, and on it everybody in town who owned a pair of skates. Old men in beards, with mufflers flying, solemnly cutting figure eights, long strings of shrieking girls sweeping by in brightly colored sweaters and long-tailed, stocking-legged caps, and big boys swooping in and out among the slower skaters, almost knocking over the stiff-backed ladies, who staggered wildly and shouted after them.

And intermingled with all this activity were no less than four games of wildcat hockey, wild, confused games without referees or rules, where it was every man for himself and the devil take the hindmost. There was a game for every age group down to the smallest toddlers. These games moved around in a most dismaying fashion, so that sometimes you found yourself playing in the wrong game. Even the goal posts were planetary, an old pair of overshoes donated by one of the players that kept sliding all over the ice, so that just when you were in position to score you would look up, and the goal would be nowhere in sight. And sometimes the game got all tangled up with the stream of skaters constantly flowing around the edge of the game like a big, slow whirlpool.

Ian sat down on the bank and began to pull at the laces of his shoes, his fingers trembling with crazy excitement.

LUMBER & WOODWORKING LTD

Hockey! hockey! greater than love, life, or fame. The excitement got into the very foot he was working on so that he had to hold it to keep it from trembling. He begrudged the few minutes necessary to put the skates on. When at last he was all ready and standing with stick in hand, like a knight of old on the edge of battle, he paused for just a moment. The slight warmth of the pale afternoon sun had melted the ice around the edge of the pond. Actually all the skaters were on an island of ice barely three quarters of an inch thick. As he watched Ian could see it swelling and sagging as the skaters gathered in one part or another, like a huge piece of billowing cloth.

He took a little run on the points of his skates, jumped over the few inches of open water, and went skimming like a bird, effortlessly, beautifully, gloriously, over the ice. He had only been skating two winters. But the right movements came to him like an instinct. He moved along, swaying, just a little uncertain on some strokes, trying not to wave his hands, trying to pretend that he had been skat-

ing from the cradle. He missed narrowly an old gentleman in the midst of a complicated figure, was almost knocked over by the sudden swoop of a couple of big boy speedsters, and went whirling and staggering completely out of control until he barged into two little girls and they all went down in a heap on the ice. It was an inauspicious start, and he hoped nobody, and especially Peebles, who was already out there somewhere, had seen him.

He headed for the group of boys his own size, some of whom he knew, but mostly strangers from all over town. For this game brought them all together in a fierce democracy, the colored boys from the hill, the French boys, the redheaded Irish, the freckled Scots, all of them. He moved through a confused conglomerate of sound—laughter, shouts, wild shrieks and squeals of dismay. But all this was drowned out as he approached the hockey game. Here was such a frantic, insane yelling that for a moment he stopped, dazed.

Instead of six players to a side there were more like fifteen in this game. He recognized Dusty playing goalie, trying half the time to keep the boots of his goal posts from floating away. Dusty *would* be playing goalie, where the puck would come shooting at him like a bullet. Ian idled up to him in a moment when the puck was being pursued by six madmen in the opposite direction. They stood side by side, watching the swarming players. Dusty was chewing gum furiously.

"You got an extra chew?" Ian shouted in his ear.

Dusty pulled off his mitten and pulled a green package of gum from his pocket. "Here, take all of it."

There were four pieces. Ian held it in his hand, pulling one piece out and slipping the others into his pocket. "Which side is behind?" he shouted.

"We are." There was a desperate look in Dusty's eyes as he answered. "Ya better get in there and score. Show them how a Quaker plays hockey!" Even as the words came out, his whole expression changed, a grim look of utter determination swept over his features, his eyes narrowed, he crouched. "Here they come!" he yelled.

And sure enough, with a wild, unearthly crying, as if the inmates of an insane asylum had broken loose, the whole thirty-odd boys came swooping down upon them, in the lead a big colored boy scooping the puck before him with his stick.

Ian's heart gave a mighty bound. The moment of destiny had arrived. There was no time even to unwrap the gum. He shoved it into his pocket. Brandishing his stick in the air, he dug his skates hard into ice and hurtled forward, gathering speed every second, his eyes fixed on the little black disk, and the whole rest of the world ignored. The colored boy flashed an astonished look at this new opponent suddenly appearing where a moment before there had been nothing between him and the goalie but ice. In his surprise he almost lost control of the puck then and there. Somehow, by a desperate contortion, he managed to catch it again with the tip of his stick. But the effort put him off balance, and at that moment, Ian came swooping in erratically, made a wild swipe at it, skidded on one skate and crashed sideways into the colored boy with a sickening thud that shook every bone in his body. Down they went together, and the next instant, like demons from hell the pack piled up on top of them.

Someone was sitting on his head, a skate was grinding back and forth over his shin bone, and his nose down flat against the ice felt as big as a potato. Gradually, however, the heap of bodies became untangled and he staggered to his feet. Someone was patting him on the back. Dazed, he turned around. It was Dusty. "Man, was *that* a body check!" Dusty cried.

All at once someone was towering over him. He looked up. It was the colored boy, his dark eyes flashing fire. "You tripped me, you son of a bitch!" he shouted. "You done it on purpose." He threw his stick down and squared off.

Ian gaped it him.

But Dusty leaped between them, pushing them apart. "What do you mean, tripped?" he yelled, almost beside himself. "That was the fairest, squarest body check I ever saw."

"Who asked for your advice?" yelled the colored boy.

"Nobody!" shouted Dusty. "You want to make something of it?" He threw his stick down and went into his famous crouch.

"I'll push your bloody teeth down your bloody throat!" the colored boy cried.

Dusty started to move in, but at that moment out of a fierce wrangle down the ice leaped a boy with the puck. Straight as an arrow he shot toward the goal. Dusty hesitated for a split second, then grabbed up his stick and tore for his deserted goalposts. The next instant both Ian and the colored player were swept away in the deluge of players. When they had all passed, he felt something warm trickling down over his lips to his chin. He put his mitten up. It came away red. His nose was bleeding. He started to reach for his handkerchief, but just then the tide of battle shifted. Two players were coming toward him, slashing simultaneously at the puck. Just as they came abreast of him, one of them fell down, and the other promptly tripped over him and went scooting along the ice on his chin. And there, unbelievably, he saw rolling on its edge, frolicsome as a kitten, the puck coming toward him.

It was no time for indecision. Gritting his teeth, he hooked the puck with the stick and started up the ice toward the waiting mass of players, friend and foe alike, all indistinguishable. Ah the thrill! Somehow he actually juggled the puck past two of them before he put his skate on someone's stick and went rolling over and over for about twenty feet, the noise fading behind him, and then, as if it loved him and couldn't leave him, the puck came skimming along beside him. He scrambled to his feet gasping. Such an opportunity might never come again. He caught the puck and began to skate madly. He gulped for air, driving his skates furiously against the ice with his last ounce of strength, and all at once he was tearing in on the goalie, who was squatting, his eyes staring, his mouth open. With a fierce hook of his stick Ian sent the puck whistling past his shoulder. He had scored!

The next instant he had crashed into the goalie, and

went whirling away like a merry-go-round on his backside away out behind the goal.

For a few seconds he lay leaning on his elbow, trying to catch his breath. He was aware of someone standing in front of him looking down at him. He looked up, and his heart leaped like a snapping mouse trap. It was Adrienne in her black reefer and white skating boots, her cheeks red as fire, her eyes black as velvet.

He gave a wan smile up into her face. Quick as a flash, before he could say a word, she dropped down on one slender knee, her eyes tender, her lips parted. "Your nose is bleeding," she said and pushed into his incredulous hand her little, snowy white handkerchief.

Automatically he pressed it against his nose, and it came away all red. "Thanks," he said, crawling to his feet. "Thanks a lot. I'll bring it back to you at school."

"Oh it doesn't matter," she said. "You can keep it if you want to. I've got lots of handkerchiefs."

He skated — no, no — he floated away from her, his legs wobbling, but in his brain a thousand Roman candles were bursting all at once.

It was dark under the stars as he limped home beside Dusty. When he stepped into the kitchen, his mother's face blanched. "Oh, my god!" she cried. "What has happened to you now?"

He glanced into the mirror over the sink and stopped appalled. There was blood crusted all over his mouth and chin and down one side of his cheek. His nose was red and swollen, his upper lip puffed out twice its normal size on one side, pulling his mouth sideways, and on his forehead was a good-sized goose egg. "I bumped into a guy on the ice, that's all," he said. "It's nothing. I scored a goal, and we won."

"Won? Who won? Who is we?"

"Why uh — we — " He stopped. Who *was* we, and which side had he been on? He remembered playing in all directions before the afternoon was over. At one time he was actually shooting the puck at Dusty.

His mother sank into a chair. "That game — I wish I could just get my hands once on the devil who invented it!"

After he had washed off the blood, he didn't look so bad, although his mouth still felt funny when he tried to smile. He sat down to the warmed up supper his mother put on the table for him and ate twelve hot biscuits with butter and maple syrup on them without stopping.

His mother fished something out of his coat pocket. "Where did you get this?" she said. "It's a girl's." She looked at him strangely.

His cheeks burned. A wild, dancing music suddenly filled the room. He stared at the little stained square of cloth in his mother's hand. "A girl gave it to me to wipe my nose."

"Oh," his mother said, "a girl gave it to you. Who was she?"

"Oh a girl called Adrienne or something like that." Her name on his own lips, spoken loud like that in the house, sounded strange and wonderful. It was almost as if she had stepped into the room.

"But you had your own — " His mother stopped

abruptly. "I hope I can get the stains out of it," she said and turned away quickly.

He reached into his pocket and pulled out his own handkerchief neatly folded and unused.

Her back was toward the door as he entered the classroom. She was talking to Burpee Oulton across the aisle; and they were laughing. He had been going to tell her about the handkerchief first thing, and now because she was laughing with Burpee across the aisle, all his determination crumpled up inside him. He slipped silently into his seat.

Miss Webb came into the room, sitting down at her desk and crossing her silk-sheathed legs. The seconds ticked by. His hands grew moist. He had to do something. Suddenly he remembered the gum Dusty had given him. Miss Webb couldn't stand gum chewing in class. It made her furious. He opened the paper wrapping under the desk and slipped the gum into his mouth.

It was several minutes before Miss Webb noticed him. She was standing by the board with an open book in one hand and a piece of chalk in the other. She was talking rapidly, and when she saw him she stopped short, as if she had walked up to a snake. She laid down her book.

"Ian McAleenan!" Her voice was stern.

He looked up at her in pretended innocence.

"Stand up."

He got up leisurely.

"What are you doing?"

"Nothing." He was aware of Adrienne's frightened face

looking up at him. A little muscle twitched in his throat.

"You are chewing gum."

"No I'm not."

Miss Webb's pretty face went a fiery red. "Now you're lying."

"I'm not chewing gum right now. I'm just holding it in my mouth."

There was a queer choking sound from Burpee Oulton and a rustling behind him.

"Put it in the basket," said Miss Webb.

He took his time, sauntering across the room to the basket in the corner. A faint smile curled his mouth as he came back to his seat. He felt as if he had walked right through a cage containing a tiger.

Miss Webb picked up her book. "The ablative," she began, "is a very curious case. Interestingly enough, it has survived — "

The class resumed its normal course.

After a while he drew out the package of gum and put a second piece into his mouth. The little muscle began to twitch again in his neck.

For a few moments nothing happened. Then all at once Miss Webb stopped again, as if she had walked up to another snake — a much bigger snake. The class grew absolutely still. They smelled blood. Somewhere a foot scraped loudly on the floor.

"Ian McAleenan!"

He looked up.

"Is that gum in your mouth?"

"Yes."

"Didn't I forbid you to chew gum?"

"No — Miss Webb."

"*What* — did you say!" Miss Webb seemed to grow a foot taller, and her big eyes began to blaze.

"You didn't say anything about not chewing gum. You just told me to put the other piece in the basket. You didn't say I couldn't chew this piece."

Miss Webb's face went red, then white, then red again. She trembled so that she had to put her hand down on the desk. Her eyes were fixed on his, and suddenly they were all alone — two strange antagonists in a mysterious duel. The excitement grew inside him. "Chewing gum is an insolent, vicious, and depraved habit — " She paused for a moment to get control of her voice, adding more quietly, "Do you have any more?"

The question caught him by surprise. "Yes," he said, scowling for the benefit of his audience.

"Put it on my desk."

He put his hand into his pocket and managed to separate one piece from the rest. He took it up and placed it on the desk. He started back for his seat.

"Stop!" shouted Miss Webb so loudly that everybody jumped in their seats. Her face was flaming. For a long moment they stood looking deeply into each other, and it wasn't hate at all that he felt — but a completely different feeling — a sweet, hollow trembling in the pit of his stomach.

"You forgot the piece in your mouth," she said with an effort.

He took the piece of gum from his mouth and started to put it on the desk.

"In the basket, please," Miss Webb said. "I don't think that piece will be of any further use to anybody."

Someone snickered.

"Quiet!" snapped Miss Webb. "This isn't funny. In fact it's rather pitiful."

But Ian didn't feel pitiful at all as he walked back to his seat.

He sat very still. He knew what he was going to do, although it wasn't at all clear to him why he was doing it. He watched the clock on Miss Webb's desk, and when there was only a minute left before the bell, he slipped the stick of gum out of its tinsel and into his mouth.

She must have been watching him out of the corner of her eye, for his hand hadn't dropped from his mouth before she said, "Ian, you go into the cloakroom." And at that moment the bell rang and everybody was so busy gathering up their books that they hardly looked at him as he went to the cloakroom. It was a bitter neglect for such a final act of daring. He stood alone and forgotten in the cloakroom, staring at Miss Webb's coat. Now he was going to get it. He was going to be strapped. He could hear her opening and slamming drawers. She was looking for the big leather strap. He heard her heels clicking sharply across the bare floor. He turned around. They were alone, facing each other in the little room.

"Hold out your hand." Her voice was low and throbbing.

He stuck out his hand, looking steadily into her face. She swung the strap down viciously. At the first blow his hand turned red as a beet. Each stroke seemed a little harder. He had never received such a strapping. He bit his lip hard to keep from crying out. Up and down went her arm. He understood that if he cried she would stop. He clamped his teeth hard together.

Then all at once she threw the strap violently into the corner, and before he could move, threw her arms around him. The smell of perfume was very strong and mingled with the faint smell of her body hot from its exertion. "Oh Ian!" She spoke softly, brokenly, her mouth almost touching his cheek. She held him tight. He was aware of the softness of her large breasts. He could feel her body trembling, and all at once he was trembling himself. Her smooth fingers cupped his chin and turned his face to her. "I'm sorry," she stammered.

It wasn't fair. He couldn't hold them back. The tears came. He sobbed once violently. The perfume grew stronger; he felt the smooth skin of her cheek brushing against his. He drew back a little, and they looked at each other. Her lips were parted; her eyes were very bright. It was a strange thing. It was as if his own mother and some strange pretty older girl, both in the same person, were going to kiss him. It was a terrible and wonderful thing. Then the strange spell snapped. Miss Webb put both hands over her face. "Oh go home," she said through her hands.

He walked home slowly through the cold, bright afternoon. He felt as if he had been on a journey to a strange land. He felt as if he had grown two years older in one afternoon.

It snowed, and the old town was all at once beautiful,

silver-gray clapboards and rich red brick against blazing white. In the afternoons the snow turned golden with long lavender shadows. For every black gaunt tree a ghostly lavender tree lay on the snow. Then it thawed and froze, and presto — the town was a crystal town with six foot icicles along the eaves, and the black trees were gold and silver trees.

It was the week before Christmas, and the word was out that the marshes were a solid sheet of ice — miles and miles of black ice. One day he startled his father right out of his chair. "Dusty and I are going into the Christmas tree business," he said.

"This is *no* year to go into any business," his father said. "By the time you have your trees hauled all the way down from the Tindale woods where will your profit be at ten cents a tree? That's all you'll get for them this year."

Ian scratched his head. "We got an idea how to do it," he said. His father said nothing.

"You know how I got my tree last year," Ian went on.

His father raised his head and looked at him for a long time. "That was only one tree," he said at last.

"We can do the same with twenty."

"One at a time?"

"No — twenty at a time."

His father pulled a long mouth. "Do you know what will happen to you? You'll end up in the Bay of Fundy — trees and all."

Ian shrugged.

"But you better think of *something* to make a little money at," his father continued, "because it's going to be

a bleak Christmas. You know I've got every cent I own and every penny I could borrow tied up in hides."

What his father said was true. The cellar, the woodshed and both sheds under the Moylan Apartments were full of hides. The farmers had been killing off their stock, and his father was swamped with hides. He had bought them fearfully. Dubious, worrying day and night, he had borrowed money from the bank and bought them. Now he hardly slept his normal three hours a night because of all the money he had borrowed. He walked around rubbing his nose, his hair in tufts about his head.

But Ian and Dusty went ahead with their plans, and finally, on a bright cold day, with a gentle northeast wind blowing in their faces, they set off on their skates up the marshes. Each had a length of clothesline and a hatchet. It was hard skating against the wind, but by two o'clock they were skimming along the creek that ran into the velvety green spruce woods. A couple of hundred yards up the creek, they came to their destination, a section of woods all grown up in young trees, packed in thick, hundreds and hundreds of perfect Christmas trees. In half an hour they had thirty-odd trees, fine bushy trees, hauled

out onto the creek, where they tied them all to each other with short bits of line. Then with Dusty at one end and himself at the other, they tugged them down the smooth ice of the creek to the open ice beyond the woods. Once out of the shelter of the woods, they were caught up by the freshening wind and began to move of their own will, at first slowly and then increasing in speed until they were skimming along at fifteen miles an hour — a strange sight on that blank expanse of ice — a great long, swaying snake of Christmas trees, with one small boy clinging to either end. It was glorious! They shouted and they sang as they went swooping down the endless expanse of ice. The little doll-like houses of the town in the distance seemed to grow before their very eyes.

Then the wind began to increase. Their speed went up and up. They tore along, their eyes watering, desperately clinging to their precious cargo. Sometimes they were flung almost together, and sometimes they almost fell. Down, down, toward the town they raced, and Ian began to wonder just how they would stop the trees when they got there.

Then it happened. Ian's skate caught in a bit of shell

ice, and flat he went on his stomach, the trees tearing from his grasp. For a few seconds he slid along helplessly and watched Dusty shooting away from him, hanging on for dear life to his big green caterpillar, now swirling madly and increasing its wild speed. It seemed to Ian that both Dusty and the trees were fairly vanishing before his eyes so swiftly did they leap away, and far away beyond them gleamed the distant silver-pink open waters of the Bay of Fundy. All at once a terrible thought came to him: Dusty would never let go of those trees. It was against all his principles to let go of them. He would ride with those trees right down the length of the marshes for five miles right into the Bay of Fundy, and that would be the last anyone would see of either Dusty or the trees.

He scrambled painfully to his feet, and with his coat held open to catch the wind set off as fast as he could toward the edge of town. As he skated, he kept his eyes on that faint whirling shadow on the ice that was the Christmas trees. He saw it go up to the edge of the town; then with a sick hollow feeling he lost it in the haze of the low sun to the west.

When at last he came up to the first houses by the marshes his legs would hardly hold him for their trembling. What terrible news he had to bring home. He sat down by the bridge over the creek and took off his skates. Starting across the bridge he heard a faint sound. He turned quickly, his heart jumping, and looked over the edge of the bridge. There on the bank, hanging upside down, with one skate caught in the tangle of slender spraying branches of an old willow stump, was Dusty. Quickly

Ian scrambled over to him and unfastened his caught skate.

Poor Dusty. His face was the color of a tomato, and on his forehead was a bump so huge that it made him look like a turtle, his nose and mouth and chin all that small and insignificant looking under his bulging forehead. As for the rest of him, he might have just come out of a threshing machine. One mitten was missing, his jacket and shirt were up under his arms, leaving his goose-pimpled belly bare to the wind, one leg of his pants was ripped from crotch to cuff, and his cap was nowhere to be seen. "Doggone it," he said, "I couldn't hold on to em. This blasted bush caught me, and I had to let go." He looked at Ian apologetically.

"That's all right," Ian said. "It wasn't your fault."

Dusty touched tenderly the bump on his forehead, and as if remembering something, blinked into the setting sun. "I wonder where they went to?" he muttered.

"They're in the Bay of Fundy," Ian said. "Come on. I'm hungry."

"Well, well," his father said, "Where are your trees?" He threw a side glance at Uncle Rufus.

"The wind was too strong. It blew them away." Ian went over to the stove and peered into the stewpot.

"Just another hare-brained scheme." His father tossed another glance at Uncle Rufus.

A few days later his father called him down cellar. "You still want to make some money?" he asked.

Ian nodded.

His father pointed to an odorous pile of black and white skins by the stone wall. "I'll give you two cents a skin to clean up those skunk pelts."

"All right," Ian said.

"I'll show you how it's done." His father picked up one of the pelts, deftly slung it onto the sloping board and began scraping off the thick fat with a sharp knife. Every once in a while he grabbed a handful of sawdust and rubbed it briskly into the leather. "Do you know the pioneers ate skunk when they got hungry?" he said.

Ian felt his stomach squirm.

"You have to be careful not to cut the skin." His father glanced at him sharply. "I'll have to fine you ten cents every time you cut through the skin." He straightened up. "Think you can do it?"

"Sure," he said.

So he went to work. The skunk pelts smelled pretty bad, but after a while he got used to it. He figured he could easily make twenty cents an hour.

In a little while his father went up the cellar steps. Just under the floor he stooped and called down. "Be careful not to get any of that skunk fat on your clothes. It has a powerful smell."

"Don't worry, I'll be careful," Ian said.

He worked away steadily. By eleven oclock he had cleaned a dozen skins. There were not more than half a dozen left — the worst ones. He picked up a particularly heavy and greasy pelt. As he worked down toward the tail he noticed what looked like a little globule of fat and gave it a quick slice with his knife. Immediately there assailed his nostrils an odor the like of which he wouldn't have believed possible. He fell back, gasping for breath. It was as if someone had poured ammonia up his nose. He dropped the knife and ran up the stairs, but he must have gotten some of that incredible effluvium on his hands, for it came right up the stairs with him. He burst out of the cellar door and into the kitchen, where his mother, who was bent over the table, straightened up as if someone had poked her in the ribs.

"Good heavens!" she cried. "Skunk! What on earth have you been doing?"

"Cleaning em," he gasped, standing helplessly, his eyes full of dismay.

His mother clapped her apron over her nose, waving with her other hand for him to go away.

But there was no place for him to go. It was winter. His father came hurrying out to the kitchen, took one breath and clapped his hand over his nose. "Great Caesar's ghost! You've cut one of the scent sacks!" he cried. Still holding his nose he strode across the room and propelled Ian toward the sink. "Where is it? On your clothes? They'll have to be burned."

"It's my hand," Ian wailed, holding up the defiled member.

"Shove it under the tap!" shouted his father. They were all shouting now. Uncle Rufus stuck his head through the door, cried, "My God!" and vanished. His father grabbed a cake of Lifebuoy soap and shoved it at him. "Scrub!" he gasped and fled for the hall door, slamming it hard behind him.

His mother had already disappeared. She had a very sensitive nose, and groaned every time a trapper showed up on the premises with a skunk. She could tell if he had just one skunk in his pack. She would shoo him and Ian's father both out to the back yard, where they did their trading in the snow. If skunk was bought, it had to be tossed into the cellar through the window, for she would never let one be carried through the kitchen.

He let the scalding water run over his hand and scrubbed with the Lifebuoy until his hand was red and raw, all with little effect. After a while his father stuck his nose through the crack in the door and told him to try a solution of ammonia. A few seconds later he stuck his head through the door again, holding out a bottle of turpentine. "Try this," he yelled and vanished.

His mother dashed into the room and deposited a bottle of Sloane's Liniment on the table. "Try that!" she cried and disappeared.

He tried them all, until he was as loaded with odors as Fuller's Drugstore, but through them all came the original taint as strong as ever.

He ate his luncheon in the cold kitchen, his mother having opened all the windows and burned tea on top of the stove, her standard antidote for skunk smell. She and the rest of the family ate in the dining room with the door closed. He felt like a pariah.

He didn't go to school the next day, but on the second day it had worn off a little, or he had just become more used to it. At any rate he decided to take the risk. He went early. There were only one or two others in the room when he entered, and for a little while after he slid into his seat nothing happened. A few more pupils came into the room, and as they entered he saw from under his forelock how their nostrils suddenly widened. Then a girl said loudly, "There's an awful funny smell in this room."

Everybody, including Ian, turned and looked at her. She blushed and bent over her books.

"Must be a dead rat between the walls," came a boy's voice.

Ian held his breath.

Adrienne came ambling in. He glanced once at that lovely face and pretended to be very busy looking for something in his desk. But he could feel his ears burning as she slipped into her seat behind him, and when he heard her restless movements, he had a sudden desire to get up and go home — but he didn't dare move now, knowing that such an act would surely expose him.

There came a rush of last-minute stragglers, the bell rang, and Miss Webb entered swiftly with an armload of books. She went directly to her desk and began calling the roll. At the second name she stopped and looked up, a puzzled expression on her face. For a long interval she looked at them, her eyes roving suspiciously. Then she bent her neat head and went on to the end of the roll call.

After she had finished, she gave them some desk work and began walking up and down all the aisles. Every once in a while she paused, and Ian knew and everyone in the class knew what had stopped her.

He heard her coming slowly down the aisle toward him. Adrienne stopped her and asked for some help. Then for a minute there was silence behind him, and then came

Miss Webb's voice: "Why of course. How could I have missed it? You forgot to square the hypotenuse." There was another pause. "Adrienne," began Miss Webb and stopped. "Never mind," she said.

She turned to Burpee Oulton, but he didn't need any help, and then Ian heard her voice above his head. "And what about you, Ian? Do you need any help?"

"I'm doin all right," he mumbled, and wondered if she could be breathing at all.

"Why you haven't done anything," she said. "Move over."

She sat down, plucked the pencil from her hair and leaning against his shoulder held the pencil out over his workbook. For a moment the perfume of Easter lilies struggled bravely in the air with that more pungent odor, then swiftly surrendered. Miss Webb dropped her pencil with a little clatter. She gave a choking gasp. She turned her head and stared at him. Then she got up so quickly she knocked a book off his desk. The book hit the floor with the sound of a gun going off. Miss Webb went up to the board, picked up her long ruler and rapped her desk with it. "I think we will have some calisthenics this morning," she said very loudly. "Reginald, will you open all the windows wide — so we may have lots of fresh air while we exercise."

Peebles jumped from his seat with alacrity, while the rest of the class clambored out into the aisles. Miss Webb put down her ruler and waited for Peebles to raise the last window, and with a stream of cool air flowing through the room, she stood very straight, so that her bosom seemed about a foot out in front of her. "Ready!" she cried in a high voice. "Eyes front *all!* Now — *arms* forward!"

The whole class shot their arms forward.

"Arms sideways," shouted Miss Webb. "Arms upward! Arms downward! Arm sideways! Arms forward!" You never knew which way she was going to call next. Arms flew in all directions. And Miss Webb in the front shot her arms this way and that like an erratic windmill.

One by one she put them through the old familiar exercises, the arms behind the neck, the touching of the floor with the fingertips, the up-and-down exercises with the hands on the hips, and the tiptoe exercises. When they had gone through them all, she said, "Now we will all breathe deeply together, filling our lungs into every crook and cranny with the good fresh air." She stretched out her arms. "Ready? Breeathe *in!*" Miss Webb's big bosom began to expand to alarming proportions, out and out it came, and then it collapsed. It was no use. Not all the open windows in the world, not all the good clean air in all the great outdoors could purify any room occupied by Ian that day.

"Breathe out," gasped Miss Webb weakly.

Everybody breathed out with enthusiasm.

"That will do. You may sit down again." Miss Webb sounded tired.

They all sat down hunching over against the cold air.

"Should I put the windows down?" Peebles asked in a small voice.

Miss Webb looked at him a little blankly. "I'm afraid we will have to put them down — " She hesitated. "Just leave them open a little bit."

When the class had quieted down, she made a motion

with her finger to Ian to come up to her desk. He stood before her miserably while she wrote something on a piece of paper. "Take this to Mr. Silliker," she said.

Ian turned and went down the hall. Mr. Silliker was the principal of the whole school, a bald-headed man, who always, as long as anyone could remember, had worn a blue serge suit. He was so efficient and energetic that everywhere he went he seemed to stir up a breeze that blew papers off desks, slammed doors and put everybody on edge. As Ian walked down the long corridor he wondered what was going to happen to him now. For nobody was sent to Mr. Silliker except as a very last resource, when all other minds had failed to solve the problem. This was the way Mr. Silliker himself insisted it should be.

Just outside the principal's office Ian unfolded the note. "Mr. Silliker," he read, "here is a special problem I am referring to you. You will understand what the problem is as soon as you receive this note." He folded the bit of paper and knocked on the door.

"Enter!" growled a deep voice.

He stepped inside. Mr. Silliker was buried in a pile of papers.

"Take a chair," he barked without looking up, and went on shuffling through the papers fiercely, licking his thumb every few seconds. Suddenly he stopped and sniffed loudly. He looked all around, under the desk, lifted one of his neat black shoes and regarded the sole, and then he looked at Ian.

"Here." Ian held out the note.

Mr. Silliker took it, eying him distastefully. He pulled out a large white handkerchief that smelled of camphor and held it to his nose while he read the note. When he had finished, he set the note down carefully and let his eye travel over Ian from head to foot.

"Where did you get that smell?" he said abruptly.

"Cleaning skunks," said Ian.

"Oh?" Mr. Silliker's voice went up sarcastically. "That must be a pleasant hobby. I'm sure the skunks must appreciate it." He put one hand on his desk. "Just how do you go about it, my young man?"

Ian brightened. "I sling em over a board," he said, "and scrape the fat off em with a sharp knife."

Mr. Silliker's eyes glazed, his mouth opened, then grew grim as a bear's. "Boy!" he said, "I am not accustomed to being played with. "Where did you get that smell?"

"Clean —"

"Boy!" shouted Mr. Silliker ominously.

"I do it for my father," Ian stammered. "My father is a fur buyer."

A light dawned in Mr. Silliker's eyes. "Oh," he said. There was a little silence as Mr. Silliker's very efficient mind grappled with the problem. At last he said, "How would you like a little holiday?"

"Very much, sir."

"Right." Mr. Silliker scribbled some words on a piece of paper. "Take this to your teacher, get your books and go home."

Ian took the paper and went to the door.

"Just leave the door open behind you," said Mr. Silliker.

As he entered, the class grew absolutely still. He felt every eye fixed on him as he walked across the front of the room to Miss Webb's desk and handed her Mr. Silliker's message. For one terrible moment as he made his way to his seat for his books his eyes looked directly into Adrienne's, beautiful and empty of expression as a summer's sky.

Very slowly he walked down Spring Street, and as he walked he tasted the dregs of shame, the bitter, bitter loneliness of the outcast. He wished with all his heart that he might never have to go back to the school again. For a wild moment he thought of persuading his parents to move to another town.

But by the end of the week, after constant scrubbings with the Lifebuoy and the further application of various astringents, the odor became so disguised and faint that only when he lifted his hand close to his face did he catch an elusive whiff of the old contamination.

When he went back to school, one or two boys started to call him Skunky, and for a few days his fate hung in the balance, but his friends stood by him. As Dusty said, "No one can call a QUAKER a skunk and get away with it."

4

IT WAS JANUARY, the beginning of the year and the death of the year, the dead center of gray, zero days numbing the body and depressing the soul of all but the young in heart. In January the men on the streets hunched over against the wind, and in the house his father walked around in his saggy sweater worrying aloud because the market in hides was falling. Uncle Rufus went away and came back. After he came back he bent for hours over sheets of paper which he filled with endless columns of figures and then tore up.

But there was hard-packed snow on the long Eddy Street hill and a pool of clean black ice where the water of the creek kept overflowing, and every night, red-faced and wet with sweat, Ian came home through the glorious gloom with Dusty and Peebles, and ate ten hot biscuits soaked in butter and maple syrup before he even began his supper.

And January was gone like the light, sharp flick of a whip.

Even when spring came, when the last dishrag patch of snow was gone from the alley corners, the grownups didn't recognize it. Spring was first an extra half hour of clear daylight after supper, when the whole world became the inside of a great melting crystal ball, cool and crisp, the sky an enormous silver dome washed with apple-green at the edges. Then in the exact center of the universe Ian sat on his front doorstep hunched over his knees. It was very still. Somewhere a dog barked, a voice called, and suddenly the clock in the Presbyterian Church struck seven long, velvet notes. Between each note like the creaking of an invisible gate up in the sky came the familiar grinding of the mechanism. High in the heavens above the glistening roofs the clock mechanism labored and whirred to make the lingering bong. Ian listened intently.

The door of the Antonelli apartment opened, and Francesca came out and sat down on her step. She leaned back against the doorpost, letting one slim, white leg dangle, and when she looked down the street, her black eyes passed over him coolly, slowly. They looked at each other across miles of space.

The street waited. The trees waited. The emerald sky waited. Francesca waited, and he waited. Somewhere a door slammed, and who but Adrienne came walking around the corner and down the street toward them, walking close to the edge of the sidewalk, her face every which way, walking as if all the windows were watching her — Adrienne in a green sweater, pale face and straight hair. She crossed the street. She and Francesca had business together. He pretended not to see them, looking up into the sky for the first star. *First star I see tonight. Wish I may, wish I might. Wish I had a million dollars. Wish I could kiss Adrienne.*

Peebles came around the corner and sat down beside him. The girls giggled softly. Suddenly out of the soft nest of their giggling came something, a murmur. It sounded like "Come on over." But it was not clear and it was not repeated. So they did not move.

But after a while Molly Manship came swinging up the street. Molly had the mysterious, dangerous, knifelike beauty of a girl of sixteen. Tall, dark, and slim-waisted with high, ripe breasts and fine legs. She stirred the men on the corners when she passed like nothing else in life. It was not just the bold, taunting look on her ravishing face that shook the men, but what was known only to the men — not yet to the women — that she was a wild girl and would go down to the marsh barns on a summer night. But what else could you expect of a girl living in that queer, inside-out house without clapboards, where you could see the plaster where it oozed through the laths because her father sold the clapboards to buy whiskey? Yet every morning, like a repeated miracle, out of that sad wreck of a home stepped this bold and beautiful creature, the rare and the perfect.

The two boys watched her from under their eyelashes.

She spoke to them of unfathomable excitement and evil. As she passed they forgot completely the two girls on the steps.

In the spring a wind blew steadily across the marshes. It was neither warm nor cold. The town stirred. The faces of the men lifted a little. And high over the town, waving and bobbing on long, invisible stems, bloomed strange triangular flowers. The men who were without work looked up at the kites and felt better. They couldn't be wholly depressed when they looked at the kites, for the kites said, "Something is going on here — something enthusiastic, energetic, and hopeful."

Always on the first fine Saturday in April there was a kite-flying contest with the stores giving prizes. This year Ian was sure he was going to win it. All he needed was a good, well-balanced kite; for the rest he had a secret.

So on Friday afternoon he set to work to make his kite, spreading out his materials, his glue and sticks and brown wrapping paper, all over the kitchen floor. He had decided on a butterfly kite, a big five-footer that would rise fast. Carefully he cut the sticks, measuring and remeasuring them, found the exact middle of the crosspiece, fastened the two sticks together, and bent the bow. The frame balanced perfectly. Then he put the frame on top of the paper and cut out the paper, turned the edges over the string around the frame and glued the edges down. By five o'clock the masterpiece was finished, and the kitchen was littered from wall to wall with bits of wood, paper and string.

His mother came in just as he was finishing. "What a

mess!" she said. "Paper and glue all over my kitchen!"

His father came into the room and held the kite up. It was so big it divided the room like a partition. "It has no tail," he said.

"Ah!" Ian exclaimed in disgust, positively swelling with disdain, "it's not a tail kite. Anybody can make a tail kite — it's a butterfly."

"Oh! a butterfly." His father looked at it more closely. "Of course. I hadn't noticed. Then, naturally, it wouldn't have a tail. What would a butterfly be doing with a tail — ha?"

"A butterfly doesn't need a tail." He was watching it in his father's hand, uneasy for fear that he might drop it with the glue hardly dry. He watched it like a mother dog watching someone lift up one of her pups.

"Isn't she a beauty!" he cried.

"Not bad." His father cocked his head critically. "But I like a tail kite. A kite doesn't seem right to me without a tail."

"A tail kite's old-fashioned." He grew impatient with his father's ignorance. "A tail kite wobbles — a butterfly is nice and steady."

He picked the kite up tenderly and carried it into the dining room, standing it in a corner where he could watch it over the rim of his soup plate as he ate his supper. He could hardly wait until the meal was over.

He was too impatient to go over to the Dowling field. He just went as far as Ely's grandfather's potato field behind Cotter's tinsmith shop. He was too excited to run in a straight line, and scampered along like a leaf in the wind, the kite swooping behind him on a couple of yards of string.

What a beauty she was! What perfect balance! He held it up high and cautiously as he climbed over the fence.

The cool evening wind swept steadily over the freshly plowed field, and he stumbled and slipped as he clambered over the furrows. He should have gone to the Dowling field. His shoes were already heavy with globs of yellow clay. He leaned the kite against a high furrow at the far end of the field so that the wind would get under it and lift it easily into the air. Then he slipped and slithered excitedly back over the furrows unwinding as he went. At last he stopped, breathing hard. Tensely he waited for a good gust of wind to lift the kite up from the ground. In a few seconds it came, pressing flat and cool against his body. He gave a little jerk of the string, and as the kite rose, started running madly, yanking the string to get the kite as high as possible before he came to the end of the field. Once he stumbled in a deep furrow full of sticky, yellow water, yet even as he fell, he kept jerking with his arm so that the kite would not lose altitude. When he scrambled up, one knee was a sticky yellow mass, and he had a great smudge on one cheek.

But clean and pure of earth's dross the kite went up straight and true. "It doesn't dive! It doesn't dive!" he sang exultantly. At last he stopped running, for the kite was now riding steadily, higher than four houses. He walked leisurely over to the fence and perched on the top railing, never once taking his eyes from the dark triangle silhouetted against the glowing evening clouds. It was a moment too full of happiness and accomplishment for words. Every few seconds he pulled slowly on the string, thrilling to feel the live thing pulling against him.

The minutes flew by. The wind was growing stronger, but he hated to reel in, couldn't bring himself to end such pure joy. Soon, however, the pull of the string in his hand became so strong that he knew he must take the kite in. He could see the wooden framework standing out strongly as the wind whipped the paper hard against it. He could even hear it slapping sharply up in the sky.

By the time he had the kite halfway in he was winding frantically, full of a sudden fear that he might lose it. The wind was blowing now in fierce gusts. He began pulling in hand over hand.

Then the awful thing happened. There was a sudden gust, the paper snapped like a gun, and a great rip appeared on one side. For a moment the kite veered wildly, and then, in a single majestic arc, dived over and downward, to crash in a tangled wreckage of paper and splints far over on the edge of the field.

Slowly he began to wind up the tangle at his feet, his eyes smarting. Why oh why hadn't he brought it in sooner? How could he win the contest now? He had no kite and there wasn't time to make another. His heart was heavy as he came up to the little heap of tattered paper and twisted sticks and kicked it.

He was a pitiable object a few minutes later, when he entered the kitchen where his mother was just taking the roast out of the oven. Cap askew, eyes red, covered with yellow mud, he trailed into the room, pulling disconsolately behind him something that vaguely resembled a wounded crane. His mother paused, holding the roasting pan between two pot lifters. She looked at him. "What a mess!" she said, softly.

His father and Uncle Rufus looked in through the parlor doors. "There's only one thing to do," said his father. "When something like this happens — you start all over again. Here is a lesson for you. Life is full of such defeats, but you mustn't give up. You must begin again — always begin again." His eye caught that of Uncle Rufus watching him with an odd expression, and he stopped short.

"Is that what you *believe,* Wallace?" Uncle Rufus asked, "or is it something you don't believe and are trying to make your boy believe?"

His father swung away. "Now if you are thinking of the shoe factory, that's a different situation altogether."

"Is it? Is it so different?" Uncle Rufus went over to a chair and sat down. "Not that it matters. Nobody else in this town has any faith in the factory either." He looked up. "I didn't tell you, did I, that I met Merrill in the post office today. 'Jim,' I said, 'the depression's been on for five years now. You can't make a pair of shoes last much longer than that even with resoling. So it's obvious everybody's going to have to buy a new pair of shoes either next year or the year following.' Do you know what he did? He just looked at me with that gimlet banker's eye of his and said, 'It'll take forty thousand dollars just to turn the first wheel.' That was what he said."

"And right he was," Ian's father said. "Forty thousand was right."

But in the morning Ian got up early and went to work again. He worked like a madman all morning, and every once in a while Uncle Rufus would come in and watch him thoughtfully. "You know you may not win this contest after all your trouble," he said.

Ian looked up at him startled. That idea just hadn't been in his head at all. He just grinned at Uncle Rufus. He knew what he knew.

Uncle Rufus sighed. "I'd like to know just how you're so sure you're going to win," he said.

The contest started at one o'clock sharp, and at twelve-thirty he was marching down the street with his precious burden. Trailing along beside him were Dusty, Peebles, Ely and Oscar. Ahead of them were three other boys carrying between them a very fancy box kite.

"Pretty," said Dusty, "but it aint beauty that counts."

"Perhaps you'll win a bicycle," said Ely.

"Fat thanthe," said Oscar. "The firth prithe latht year wath a Book of Knowledthe thet." He gave a snort of disgust.

"Heck, it's winning that counts," said Peebles. "THE QUAKERS will show them."

He didn't say anything. Just kept his eyes on his kite. Anything might happen — a branch might just fall from a tree. It might bump into a telephone pole.

When they arrived at the field it was almost time to start. The big field was full of boys running in all directions, and around the edge, leaning against the iron railing, were about two hundred grownups. Along the far side of the field there was already a line of boys holding up kites from which ran strings to the hands of the proud owners. There seemed to be every kind of kite in the world there. Box kites, barrel kites, even an old tail kite, and one enormous ten-foot-high kite.

"Say! You forgot your string!" Peebles cried suddenly.

"I got something to show you," Ian said, and he reached inside his shirt and pulled out an object — it was a large spool of very fine, very strong shoemaker's thread that he had found in the factory. "It's twice as strong as string and twice as light," he said, "and there must be a mile of it on this spool."

For a long time Peebles stared at it; then he uttered a low whistle. "Boy oh boy!" he said, and looked at the others. He rubbed his hands together. "Come on. Let's get it fastened onto the kite."

Ian was so excited that when the gun went off he jumped like a hare. Across the field Peebles shot the kite up into the air, everyone uttered a shout, and then he was running with the other contestants, all looking over their shoulders as their kites went up.

When all the kites were about two hundred feet up, the big ten-footer suddenly took a tremendous dive, tangling

with the strings of half a dozen others, bringing them all down to earth. It missed Ian's line by a hairbreadth. When that excitement had died down, someone discovered what looked like a miracle; for the thread to Ian's kite being practically invisible, it looked as if his kite were hanging in the sky without any attachment. "Look! Look!" the cry went up. "That kite hasn't got any string!"

They crowded around him, staring at the big spool of shoemaker's thread spinning smoothly as he held it on a stick between his hands. There were some cries of "Unfair," but the judges just laughed and said there were no rules against using thread, or anything else that would hold a kite.

First prize would be won by the kite that reached the greatest height in twenty minutes. The problem was to let out the greatest amount of string without your kite losing altitude. All over the field stood boys with their torpedo-shaped spools of white string jerking at their feet like big bugs. But held down by the increasing weight of their long, looped string, the other kites were at a distinct disadvantage. Ian's kite, with its feather-light thread whirling evenly from its spool, literally climbed up into the heavens. At the end of twenty minutes, the judges began trying to figure out which kites were the highest with the help of a surveyor's tripod.

Ian waited complacently. It was hardly a contest at all. Even with the naked eye it was obvious that his kite had outclimbed them all. He glanced over to where the judges were talking. Suddenly he saw them coming toward him.

"All right, my boy," said the head judge, a wide smile

on his face, "you can stop letting her out. You've won first prize. Now if you will come over —"

His words were drowned out in the cheer from the crowd. Ian's heart jumped, and at that moment his hand felt suddenly light. He looked down at the spool. It was still spinning, but there was no more thread on it. He glanced across the field. A little white tab on the end of the thread was vanishing toward the distant fence with huge leaps, like some kind of super grasshopper.

There was only one thing to do. He leaped madly after it, leaving the judges and the crowd staring after him with open mouths. The shouting died away behind him. Looking once over his shoulder, he saw Dusty and Peebles tearing after him.

Already the thread was strung across the roof of the haunted house across the road from the field. For a moment it looked as if it had caught in the eave, but the next instant it broke loose again and went running over the open fields toward the distant black shadow of the woods. And over the rail fence the three of them went after it. Over the fence and across the fields; over ditches, bushes, rocks, over and under more fences, barb-wire fences. They ran right through a brook, almost got caught in Dickie's Swamp, and scrambled through a bunch of alders. They could no longer see the tab at the end of the thread. They watched the kite. Then Dusty and Peebles dropped behind, out of wind, and he was panting on alone. He wondered why the kite was still up in the sky at all. At last, when he couldn't have run another ten yards, he came upon the thread entangled in a thornbush. Far out in the country the kite rode serenely in the sky.

By the time he had wound it in again and walked back to the playfield, everyone had gone home but Ely. Even Dusty and Peebles had vanished. He sank down on a bench.

"Your prize is over there," Ely said, "leaning against the boiler room."

Ian raised his head wearily. It was dusk and he couldn't see very clearly. He got up and walked toward the brick wall of the boiler room. Then he saw what it was and his knees went all weak, and two smarting tears came into his eyes, for it was a big, gleaming red bicycle, a thing so remote from all possibility that he had long ago given up even dreaming about owning one.

"Well, well, how did you make out?" His father regarded him gloomily as he stepped into the kitchen.

"Not bad."

"I know. You don't need to tell me." His father nodded sagely. "You probably won third prize — a book on how to make a kite."

Uncle Rufus came into the room and watched him.

"It's outside," Ian said. "You can see it against the shed in the light of the kitchen window."

The two men went over to the window.

After a long time his father said in an oddly chastened voice, "Is that it?"

"Yes," he answered. His heart swelled inside him.

"You see," Uncle Rufus said slowly, and nobody could tell whom he was talking to, "you've got to have faith. *You've got to have faith.*"

"Ah, faith!" His father cried out in bitter anguish. "I'll tell you when that old factory will start up again — when the lions feed the tigers." He stomped out of the room.

5

MR. MERRILL the banker came to the house. He talked with Uncle Rufus in the parlor behind locked doors for an hour. Ian could hear their voices, sometimes low, sometimes high. When the banker was gone, Uncle Rufus came out looking wild-eyed and haggard. He looked at Ian's father. "It's come," he said, "the final ignominy."

"What's come?" his father asked.

"Mooney the junk dealer has offered Merrill four thousand dollars for the shoe factory, and he wants to sell it."

Ian's father put down the paper. "Is Mooney going into the shoe business?" he asked incredulously.

"No!" Uncle Rufus shouted. "He wants the factory for junk. He's going to dismantle the machines and sell them for junk. He's going to tear down the building and sell the bricks." He began striding back and forth, striking his hands together, his face white. "My whole lifework! All gone to junk. Junk! Junk!" He stopped short and stared at them. "We've got to do something, Wallace."

His father was silent.

"B.J.'s got money. Father's got money. Father's got twenty thousand dollars in the bank right now, earning two per cent. Old Merrill's making four per cent off of it!"

"Don't look at me," his father said. "I've got no money."

"You've got hides. You've got about five ton of fine calfskin hides."

"Raw hides," his father said, "not tanned."

"We can get them tanned. Old Janfer will tan them on credit for me."

"You're crazy, Rufus. Plain crazy."

"I'm going to write a letter to Harrison. Harrison and I did business together for fifteen years. He knows the shoe market like nobody else in the country. I'm going right up to my room and write to him now." He turned and stomped out of the kitchen.

"I won't let you talk Father out of his life's earnings," Ian's father shouted after him.

But a week later Uncle Rufus came bursting into the house waving a letter. His hat was over one ear, and his face was flushed. "Listen!" he shouted. "Just listen to this. It's from Harrison." He opened the letter with shaking hands and ran his finger down the page. "Listen now." He began to read. "But Rufus, if you can send me a sample Forshay shoe, I'm pretty sure I can get you an order with a big distributor. There is a market opening for that type of shoe. But I'd have to be able to show him the shoe —" Uncle Rufus looked up. "There!" he exclaimed.

"Rufus," his father said slowly. "You've lost your mind."

"And *you've* lost your spirit. You won't even take a chance any more. What's happened to you? I remember the time when you'd be all on fire at a chance like this. I remember when *you* would take the lead."

"I was younger then." His father chewed fiercely the end of his mustache.

"So you were younger. Does that make you an old man? My God!" Uncle Rufus paced about the room.

"There's a depression, Rufus. Haven't you heard? There's been a depression for five years."

"Well, I'm not going to let that factory be torn down for junk." Uncle Rufus slapped his hat onto his head. "I'm going to have one more talk with Merrill. I'm going to have a talk with B.J." He strode over to the door.

"And where are you going to find a new pair of Forshay shoes?" Ian's father called out.

Uncle Rufus stopped short. "I'll find a pair somewhere," he shouted. "There must be a pair somewhere." He yanked open the door and rushed out, slamming it so hard that the barometer fell off its nail. Ian went over and picked it up. He looked at his father. "I guess I'll go out for a while," he said.

Outside, he rushed over to Peebles' house. "Come on," he said when Peebles answered the doorbell. "We're going over to the shoe factory."

Peebles' eyebrows went up. "What we goin there for?"

"You remember the shoe still in the machine?"

Peebles scratched his head. "Oh yeah. I remember."

"Well, we're going to finish it."

"Then we better get Dusty," Peebles said.

They stood looking down at the shoe. Ian wiped the dust from it with his sleeve. Dusty had his head to one side. He put his hand out to the wheel and moved it back and forth a little. "You turn this wheel and the needle moves up and down," he said. "All we gotta do is turn the wheel." He leaned on it. "Only it turns kind of hard."

Peebles picked up a bar of iron and inserted it between the spokes. "Now all together," he said.

They all leaned on the bar. The wheel turned, the needle went down and came up.

"Jumpin junipers! We made a stitch!" Ian's voice crackled with excitement.

"All together again!" cried Peebles.

They made five stitches, and the shoe was done. Dusty cut the thread with his knife, and Ian lifted the shoe from the machine. He turned it around. It looked fine. He turned it over and squinted at the sole — and there it was in flowing brown letters: FORSHAY.

When he came back into the kitchen with the box under his arm, Uncle Rufus was sitting by the window looking out. "Here's something for you." Ian held out the box, aware of his father watching him from the hallway.

Uncle Rufus looked at him and then down at the box. Silently he took it and unwrapped it. Silently he lifted out the beautiful shoe, all polished until it shone like glass.

Ian waited, very proud.

Then all at once Uncle Rufus jumped up from his chair and rushed out of the room, his face working as if he were going to sneeze. Ian regarded him with astonishment. "What's wrong?" he asked his father.

His father shook his head. "He's had a hard day," he said.

"You mean Merrill and B.J. aren't going to put up the money?"

"Nobody," his father said. "Nobody in town is going to put up the money. Nobody believes in miracles."

But next morning Uncle Rufus came down, looked at the shoe still sitting on the window sill, clamped his hat on his head and went out with his chin set like a vise. All week he went about town trying to find some capital. He even wrote a letter to the paper. He got the whole town buzzing and uneasy, but at the end of the week he was discouraged again. "Those that haven't the money are all for the idea, and those that have aren't. The town is dead, and dead it will stay until grass grows in Main Street and they plow it under. Nobody, nobody can say I didn't try. I've done my duty. Now the rats can take over. Give it all to Mooney." He waved an arm dramatically.

Nobody said a word, not even Ian's father.

6

THAT WAS THE DAY Dusty began talking about the Klondike. He came around on the old bicycle he had constructed out of parts from Mooney's junkyard. For over two years he had been working on it, and there were still a few things missing, like mudguards and a seat. But the lack of mudguards merely gave it a racy appearance, and the seat problem he solved by tying on a pillow with some rope. But that was only for long trips. Most of the time he went around without any sort of seat, standing on the peddles, going up and down in a peculiarly disjointed fashion that made him look like a wooden marionette. "Good for the leg muscles," he would exclaim.

"Who wants to go fishing?" he cried out cheerily.

"Where would you go fishing?" Ely said.

"Me Uncle Hazen knows a stream about eight miles from town." Dusty leaned his bicycle against the woodshed, looked at it for a moment lovingly, and sat down on the steps. "Me Uncle Hazen says there used to be the best fishing in the county there when he was a boy."

"What's the name of it?" Ian's voice wavered between indifference and mild interest.

"The Klondike."

"Ah, I've heard about that stream," Ely said scornfully. "It's no good."

"Me Uncle Hazen says it is." Dusty looked at Ian.

Ian shrugged. "Okay. Why not?"

"It's eight miles," Ely said.

"We got bikes." Dusty glanced at the gaunt frame leaning against the fence.

"I aint."

"What about your aunt?" Ian said.

"What! Me ride a girl's bike?" Ely looked pained.

"For cripes sakes," Dusty said. "You're gonna be out in the country. Nobody's gonna see you. Now let's see. We can cut alders for poles, and I got some fishline, but we need hooks. You got any hooks?"

"Who — me?" Ely said.

"Let's go over to my Uncle B.J.'s store," Ian said. "He's got everything."

B.J. was leaning over the counter talking to old Cotter the tinsmith when he saw them coming, and he automatically reached out and put the cover over the cheese.

They stood around for a while looking at the chocolate bars.

"What do you want, boys?" B.J. said.

"We thought you might like to make some money," Ian said.

"Well, I've certainly no objections to that." B.J. threw a glance at old Cotter.

"We need some fishhooks —"

"Gottem." B.J. straightened up. "How many?"

"Oh about ten."

B.J. put the box of fishhooks on the counter. They were all tangled together, and when he tried to separate them he pricked his finger. "Judas!" he exclaimed. "For half a penny's profit! Here, take these things, and don't all lean at once on that counter. The hooks will be five cents."

"We figured on paying for the hooks with fish," Ian said.

B.J. stared at him.

"We'll give you one fish for each hook," Ian went on. "You can sell them for five cents each and make forty-five cents clear."

"Forty-five and a half cents," said Ely.

"Ha!" B.J. stared at Ely. "Where do you think you're going to find ten fish around here? I know for a fact that there isn't a single solitary trout in this whole damn county. Every damn fish was eaten up in the last depression." He turned to old Cotter. "That was when the Conservatives were in, you remember, Joe?"

"Me Uncle Hazen knows a place, though." Dusty leaned a little forward and the counter creaked ominously.

"The counter," B.J. said quickly.

"And was yer Uncle Hazen sober, boy, when he told you of this place?" Old Cotter cackled.

"Look, boys," B.J. said. "I don't like to disappoint you, but everybody knows there's no fish around here. You're just kids. You got big ideas, but we know. We been around a bit longer than you have. Why, I've had this box of fishhooks for five years."

"It's all the lumberin that killed the fish," Old Cotter said. "Sawdust."

"So save yourself a lot of trouble, boys." B.J. shoved the hooks back into the box. "You ought to be working on Saturdays — big fellows like you."

"We'll work for you *next* Saturday if you'll give us the hooks," Ian said.

B.J. paused with the box in the air. "All three of you?"

They nodded.

"Well, that's different." He put the box on the counter. "Take your ten hooks."

As they went out through the door, Old Cotter stood up and spread his hands out over the cold stove. "You can't reason with young fellows," he said.

"What do we do now?" Ely said.

"What do we do? We dig worms," Dusty said.

"You mean you're still going on this crazy trip?"

Dusty looked at Ian. "Me Uncle Hazen —"

"Ah — your Uncle Hazen!" Ely exclaimed. "B.J. and old Cotter — they ought to know."

But Ian stared off into the distance. He saw the sour, screwed-up face of old Cotter, gray as death, and something inside him rebelled. It wasn't just a question of fish. They were the same way about the shoe factory. The shoe factory might succeed, and there just might be fish in the Klondike. "Let's go and dig the worms," he said.

In the morning when the old alarm clock went off, Ian leaped for it with both hands before it could dance off the table. Rubbing his eyes he groped his way to the bathroom and doused his head in a basin of cold water. Down in the empty kitchen he shook some cornflakes into a bowl and poured the top of the milk over them. Behind him heavy steps clomped down the stairs, and his father appeared in the doorway, his hair up in tufts all around his head. It looked like a crown, but his father didn't look like any king with his undershirt half in and half out of his pants.

"What in thunderation are you doing up at this hour?" his father said.

"Going fishing."

His father went over to the stove and lifted the lid. "Where?" he asked.

"Oh, we know a place."

His father put the lid back on the stove. Hunched over and aimless he stood among the shadows of the kitchen, his eyes bleak, the corners of his mouth pulled down. "You might as well stay home," he said. "The streams are all fished out."

"Dusty's Uncle Hazen says there's fish in this stream for sure."

"You'd do better to stay home and shovel the winter ashes out of the cellar. I'd give you something for that. I might even go as high as ten cents for a good job."

"I'll do it next week, Pop." He gulped his milk and edged toward the back door.

His father pushed his hands into the hollow of his back in a futile effort to straighten it. "The world is full of failures who have used that expression." He spoke sternly. "Now, when I was a boy —"

But Ian was gone, running his bicycle along the driveway and leaping into the saddle without touching the stirrups — Tom Mix with a dozen bandits after him.

Dusty and Ely were waiting for him at the corner, and together they rode off along Main Street and out into the country, where the red sun, big and close, rolled along with them behind the gnarled birches that lined the road. In the trees and brush a million birds twittered.

Later in the morning they stopped at a weatherbeaten farmhouse for a drink. The farmer himself caught the crystal-clear water from the pump in an old tin cup. As they drank, he stood among the scratching hens rubbing the back of his hand across the stubble on his chin.

"Town boys?"

"Yes." Ian wiped his mouth with his sleeve. "We been riding all morning."

"Thought so. Nothing to do but ride around on bicycles."

"Guess we musta come about nine mile," Ely said.

"Five."

They looked at him incredulously.

"Five miles to town." He took back the cup. "Fishin?"

"Yep," Ely said.

"No fish around here. City folk grabbed them all up."

"We're going to try the Klondike," said Dusty.

"No fish there. None for years. Sawdust killed them." His eyes traveled over their faces solemnly.

"Well, we might as well try, since we came this far," Dusty said. "How much farther is it, anyhow?"

"A mile and a half to old Harvey's farm and about two miles through the woods."

They picked up their bikes. "What's the Harvey farm look like?"

The farmer was already bending over a piece of harness. "Fallin down." He didn't look up. "All fallin down around old Harvey's head."

At the foot of the hill beyond the farmer's field the road turned into a dappled tunnel through old spruce trees, with tall, pungent weeds filling the ditch. They rode on for about twenty minutes until they came to a hillocky field surrounded on all sides by the spruce trees. In the center of the field was a house so decrepit that it looked as if all the boards were just propped against each other — none of them nailed. Beside it a barn leaned so far to the south that it seemed a miracle the walls didn't collapse. A cow the color of an old pipe bowl stood among the thistles. When it moved, a bell around its neck tinkled faintly.

"This must be it," Ely said.

At that moment they saw the old man. He was sitting in an antique rocking chair watching them. At least he seemed to be watching them. His face, mostly covered with a long, yellowish beard, was turned in their direction.

They pushed their bicycles up the path toward the house. The old man didn't move, and when they came up close they saw that he was sitting in the rocker, bolt upright, his eyes closed, his face expressionless.

"Hey — Mister!" cried Ely.

The old man didn't move.

"Perhaps he's dead," Ian suggested.

"More likely he's deaf," said Dusty. "Let's all shout together. One two three —"

"Hey!" They all roared at the top of their lungs.

The old man gave a little jerk and started rocking quietly back and forth. After a while he opened his faded blue eyes, saw them standing in a row in front of him, and let his toothless, round mouth fall open with surprise. He stopped rocking.

"Can we leave our bicycles in your yard for a while?" Dusty shouted.

The old fellow nodded. "Catch any fish?" he asked in a high squeak, his eyes on their baskets.

"We haven't started yet. We're going back to the Klondike." Ian leaned forward and shouted.

The old man nodded again. "Good fishing there."

"See!" Dusty turned on them. "I told you me Uncle Hazen —"

"About ninety. Lots of trout back in ninety. None now. Sawdust killed em all off." The old man began to rock again.

Dusty stared at him.

"I'm hungry," Ely said. "Why don't we eat right here? Then we won't have to carry all this grub any more."

"We'll have to carry it just the same," Dusty said.

"Mind if we eat on your lawn?" Ely yelled at the old man.

The old fellow nodded, watching them with something almost like a gleam of humor in his little red-rimmed eyes.

They sat down on the close-cropped grass and began to eat hungrily. Above them the old man's chair creaked rhythmically, and in the field the cow bell tinkled softly.

"Shouldn't we offer the old guy something?" Ian said.

Dusty jumped up at once and stepped over to the veranda, a sandwich in his extended hand.

The old man reached out slowly. He raised the sandwich close to his face. "Boughten bread," he said. He opened it up carefully. "Meat," he said. He laid the sandwich down on his knees and began picking the meat apart into tiny bits, popping them one after the other into his mouth and smacking his lips noisily.

Down on the grass they watched him. When he had finished the sandwich, Ian took him a piece of rhubarb pie.

The old fellow's eyes shone, and his head began to shake like a gray dandelion in the breeze. "Pie," he said. He put his nose down close and sniffed for a long time. Finally he looked down at them. "Rhubarb," he said as if he had made some remarkable discovery.

They looked at each other, their eyes dancing with laughter.

When they had all finished, the old fellow got up very slowly and stomped through the open door. After a moment he came out again with a flat, black bottle in one hand and a pitcher of water and a cup in the other. The cup dangled by the handle from his little finger and as his hand trembled, the cup beat a little rat-a-tat against the side of the pitcher.

"Have a drink," he said.

They were startled, wondering if his eyesight was so bad that he had mistaken them for grown men. They lined up along the veranda, excited and curious, while he bent slowly over and set the cup and pitcher and bottle all in a row along the edge. He tottered a little as he came up, and Ian put out his hand to keep him from falling.

Ely sniffed the mouth of the bottle. He looked up at the old man. "What is this stuff?" he shouted.

"Applejack, sir. Made it myself. No better drink."

"How do you make it?"

"Make it? Did you say make it? Why, freeze hard cider and drain off the juice. Best drink in the world."

"What's the water for?" Ely yelled.

"Cool you off afterward." The old fellow sank down into his chair with a sigh.

They stared at the three vessels and then at each other. Never before had anyone offered them a drink of hard liquor. Ian looked up. The pale blue eyes were watching him intently. He stepped forward, picked up the black bottle, put it to his mouth and, shutting his eyes, tilted it recklessly. The next instant he felt as if someone were shoving a red-hot poker down his throat. Choking and gasping he grabbed the pitcher of water, not bothering with the cup, slopping the water all over his jacket as he tried to put out the fire in his throat.

The old fellow slapped his thigh. "Hot," he said.

Dusty, who had never backed out of a dare in his life, reached for the bottle. "Guess I'll mix mine," he said nonchalantly, and poured a third of a cup of the liquor, filling the rest with water. He stirred the mixture with his finger and gulped it down quickly, making such a terrible face in his effort to keep from coughing and turning such a fantastic shade of orange, with the black spots of his freckles standing out, that they couldn't take their eyes off him. Finally Ely followed him, and just to show what sterner stuff he was made of, Ian followed Ely, and because, as always, nobody could be braver than he, Dusty followed Ian, and because —

The old fellow rocked back and forth above them. "Have another," he said cheerfully.

They tried it just once more. Then Dusty said they better be moving along if they were going to catch any fish before nightfall. Very solemnly they thanked the old man and started over the field toward the pole gate that marked the beginning of the wood road.

"Feel anything yet, anybody?" Ely asked as they tramped over the grass.

"Nah," Ian said, but he wondered a little if the field was really as wavy as it appeared; he seemed either to be pounding his foot too hard against the earth or reaching for it as it dropped away. Suddenly the top of the hill rolled right by him like a wave, and he was sitting down. He laughed. He hadn't intended to sit down in the middle of the field at all. That's what made it so funny.

"I feel fine myself," Ely said, looking at him strangely, and all at once he opened his mouth and started to sing, "Oh the old gra-a-ay ma-a-are, she aint what she used to be, aint what she used to be —"

Ian got up unsteadily. He seemed to be leaning sideways, and they all ran staggering down the hill together singing, "Oh the old gray mare, she pooped on the whippletree! pooped on the whippletree!" And as they ran, their fishbaskets banged against their backs and their alder poles waved wildly in the air. They climbed over the gate and set off helter-skelter down the damp wood road. Every so often one of them staggered and sat down with a thump on a green moss pillow. When that happened, they all laughed uproariously, scaring the wits out of the squirrels. Once Ian stumbled into a spruce tree. "Begga pardon," he said to the tree, and they laughed for five minutes without stopping. The squirrels followed them scolding hysterically.

"All right, Mama," Ely said to one little fellow up on his hind legs on a log. "I won't do it again."

Dusty bellowed and the squirrel vanished.

At last the wood road dipped down and down into green foliage as if it were going to the bottom of the earth, and there, suddenly, through the branches was the glitter of running water. The sight of it filled them with a mad fever to be fishing, as if all the fish might swim away before they could get their hooks baited. They tore down that steep and dangerous slope and in no time at all were bent over the water like three statues, poles held out, lips pursed, eyes glued on their lines. They waited motionless so for two whole minutes. Then Dusty said, "This spot's no good. I'm going downstream."

"It looks better upstream," Ian said.

Dusty looked at him. "Me Uncle Hazen said *downstream.*"

They went downstream, stumbling along the bank, catching their toes in the snakelike roots of the trees. All at once Ely uttered a cry. "A raft! A raft!" and following his pointed finger they saw a crude raft of boards and logs among the alders.

"There you are," said Dusty. "The right way to fish is

out on the water." He was already down on the ground pulling off his shoes and stockings.

They crept onto the wobbly craft cautiously. Some of the logs when you stepped on them went slowly down into the water. "It's just like a submarine," Ian exclaimed.

"Can you guys swim?" Ely asked uneasily.

"Sure, sure," Dusty said. He had grabbed up an old birch pole. "You fish and I'll pole," he shouted generously.

They stood with legs braced, balancing precariously as the dubious craft floated away from the bank. Whenever two of them got close together the raft tipped dangerously. Suddenly the current caught them and away they went swinging around and around.

"Man alive! This is the life!" Ely cried, his eyes shining.

"Ahoy you landlubbers!" Ian cried to the trees. He staggered, stepped on a loose log and went down to his knees.

At that instant Dusty uttered a cry of warning. Ian got a brief glimpse of a great gray boulder splitting the water ahead of them, then there was a jolt, and the raft disintegrated into separate floating logs and boards. Head first he went into the icy stream, thrashing wildly, sure he was going to drown, knowing with awful clarity that he could swim no more than three dog-paddle strokes. After an age his feet touched bottom; he kicked wildly and straightened up, realizing that the water was only up to his waist. But it was swift water, spinning him about, pulling him over again gasping, banging him against something hard. Then all at once he was standing on a

sandy bottom in a quiet little cove with a blue jay scolding over his head. He heard a cry for help and turning around saw Ely caught in a tangle of driftwood, water up to his neck, thrashing his hands. "Do something quick," he cried. "Something's got hold of me. I think it's an octopus."

But here Dusty came wading out of the shadows thrusting out his pole. "Grab this," he said with magnificent calm, and when Ely had grabbed it, Dusty and Ian pulled with all their strength.

"Hurry," Ely bleated, "it's pulling me under."

"All together," said Dusty, and they pulled and Ely shot out of the water with such abruptness that both Dusty and Ian went over backward. When they recovered themselves, Ely was wading toward them with an unhappy look on his face, and when they had all crawled onto the bank, they understood why. He had lost his pants.

"Holy catfish!" shouted Dusty, and he and Ian rolled over on the moss, beating it with their hands at the sight of Ely in his wet underdrawers.

"Did you see that thing that had me?" Ely asked.

"Yeah," Dusty said. "It was a root."

"Root nothing." Ely surveyed his goose-pimpled legs. "How'm I going to get home? I can't go back through town like this."

"Aw, we'll think of something," Dusty said grandly. He began taking off his own dripping clothes and wringing them out. In a few seconds all three of them were standing white and naked among the trees, their clothes festooned over the branches to dry.

"Well," said Dusty, "we still got our poles, and I've got

some bait. We might as well fish. That's what we came for."

"If you ask me," said Ely, "this has been one heck of a fishing trip." He reached into the can for a worm. "So far I've almost got drowned, lost my pants, and haven't got a bite."

"We'll have one more try," Dusty said, "and if nothing happens, we'll pack up and go home."

They baited their hooks and walked along the bank. They came to a place where the stream spread out over thick water cress.

"Maybe the trout like that grass," Ely said.

"Aw, nuts," Dusty snorted. "Trout like deep holes, everybody knows that."

But Ely stopped and cast his line at the water. It hit the water with a little plop. It seemed to Ian that it had barely touched the water before Ely jerked it into the air with a silver-bellied trout wiggling on the hook. They stared with unbelieving eyes at the fish — it might have been the Holy Grail.

"Boy, oh boy," cried Dusty and threw in his line. Ian followed, and no sooner did their lines hit the water than there came that glorious tug, and they each pulled out a wiggling ten-incher. By that time Ely had another fish flying through the air. There never was such fishing! As fast as they could bait their hooks and drop them into the water the trout took them. They stood in the middle of the stream like naked dryads, fishing madly. As they walked down the stream they shouted out their tallies. "Thirteen!" shouted Ely. "Twelve!" cried Dusty. "Fifteen!" yelled Ian.

"And whattya think of me Uncle Hazen now?" cried Dusty.

They used up all their worms and kept right on fishing with trout eyes. It seemed that those trout had been starving all their lives. The baskets grew heavy, but they couldn't stop. When their baskets wouldn't hold any more fish, they pulled off branches and strung their catch on the branches. When they finally did give up, they found that Ian had sixty-three trout, Dusty sixty-five and Ely seventy-seven.

Gaily they put on their damp, wrinkled clothes and started on the long walk back through the woods. Ely, naked from the waist down except for his underdrawers and his boots, looked like some kind of witch doctor with a garland of trout around his neck. Every two minutes he would shift his burden and utter a groan. "Ohmygod," he would cry, "how much farther is it?"

"Whatsa matter?" Dusty would say. "All you gotta do is throw away a few trout."

But they knew they wouldn't throw away a single trout if they had to crawl the last mile home on their hands and knees.

When they finally came around the corner of the old house in the field, there was the old man still asleep in his rocker just as they had first seen him. All through the last four hours of their glorious excitement he had slept on in his chair.

"Hey!" they all shouted together.

He opened his red rimmed eyes and stared at them. "Goin fishing?" he squeaked.

"We *been* fishing!" Ely yelled.

"No fishin hereabouts." The old fellow shook his head.

"We been fishing in the Klondike!" Dusty yelled.

"No fish in the Klondike since ninety." The old fellow began rocking again.

"Then whattya call this?" Ely stepped to the edge of the veranda and opened the cover of his basket.

The old man stopped rocking and began to tip forward. For a long time he continued to tip forward, staring at the trout, his mouth open. After a while his little eyes came up and looked at their faces, then dropped down to the fish again.

Ian and Dusty opened their baskets and set them beside Ely's. The old man's head moved back and forth like a bucket on a stick. He looked frightened. "It's that apple-jack," he said at last under his breath.

"Applejack nothing!" Ely spluttered. "Them's real fish."

The old fellow looked at him and his pale eyes glinted briefly. "I suppose them's real pants yer wearin — too." He pointed a shaky hand at Ely's skinny thighs.

Dusty snorted.

"That's what we woke you up for," Ian shouted. "He wants to trade some fish for an old pair of pants."

"Got no pants but these here pants." The trembling, spotted hands plucked at the faded overalls stretched across the bony knees.

Ely's face fell. He looked at them desperately.

"Got an old flour sack," came the quavering voice.

"What's the good of that?" said Ely petulantly.

"All I wore till I was ten year old, young feller."

"Better take it," Dusty said. "You can get arrested going around like that."

The old man pushed himself to his feet, reached through the open door and pulled out a dusty, faded sack with PRIDE OF THE GOLDEN WEST printed in large red letters on one side. He drew from his hip pocket an enormous knife, but when he unclasped it the blade, they saw, had been honed down to a little thin point of steel barely an inch long. They stared at the strange knife as he sawed a hole in either bottom corner of the sack. From a little pile on the veranda he picked out a short piece of cord. He handed the cord and the sack to Ely, who reluctantly put his legs through the holes and tied the top about his waist. They eyed him critically. He looked like a skinny, oversized baby in rompers, and when he turned around, there was PRIDE OF THE GOLDEN WEST in big red letters on his backside. Ian looked at Dusty. For a moment their faces twisted in all directions, then they exploded into hoots of laughter.

Ely stared at them coldly.

"About three of them trout would make a nice mess for me," the old man said.

As they wheeled their bikes out through the gate, they turned to look back. The old man was already sitting bolt upright again in the rocking chair with his eyes closed.

"He must sleep all the time," Ian said.

It was all right riding back until they came to Embree's ice pond. Then the west wind from the Bay of Fundy hit them head on. They had to stand up on the pedals to keep moving, and the baskets on their backs seemed to be full of stones. Every few minutes Ely would groan, "Oh-mygod, I'll never make it."

"Throw away your trout!" Dusty would shout over his shoulder.

But they finally did make the town, and to the merry music of the six o'clock whistle of the coffin factory they rolled down Main Street. The people hurrying along the sidewalks glanced at them, caught sight of Ely's strange appearance and stopped to follow them with their eyes. Ely looked neither to right or to left.

As they rounded the corner of Fuller's Drugstore, Ian saw B.J. hurrying home. He pulled up to the curb beside him. "You wanta buy some fish, B.J.?" He swung the basket around to his side and opened the cover. Dusty and Ely stopped beside him and opened their baskets.

B.J. stared down at the fish. For a long time his eyes took on that narrow look he always got when he thought somebody was putting something over on him. "You caught all those trout in a brook?" he said at last slowly.

"That's right," Ely said.

B.J.'s eye traveled over Ely, coming to a stop on his flour-sack pants, and for once B.J. didn't seem sure of himself. He looked around. He put his hand on the arm of the man beside him. "Do you see those fish?" he asked.

The man nodded, grinning.

"I just wanted to make sure. For years everybody around here has been saying that there were no trout left — no trout."

"That's right," the man said. "The streams are all fished out everybody said."

"But there they are," B.J. said, and all at once he was smiling. It was a silly, uncomfortable-looking smile, but it was a smile, and an astonishing thing, because if Ian hadn't known it was B.J. smiling like that he would never have recognized him — it changed him that much.

It made him feel quite funny about B.J., like wanting to tell him about the time he and Ely had stolen the sauerkraut from his back shop, but by now a regular little crowd had gathered about them looking in astonishment at the three heaping baskets of fish.

A short fat man leaned forward with a pencil and notebook in his hands. "How about a story for the *Daily News,* boys?"

"Nothin much to say." Dusty stuck out his chest. "We just caught sixteen dozen trout. What's so wonderful about that?"

"Where?" several excited bystanders cried.

"Oh we're not saying where," Ely said quickly.

Everyone looked at him, and his face turned the color of a ripe tomato.

"What did you use for bait — yer pants?" someone called.

The crowd roared.

"Sure musta made good bait," came another voice.

"Let's get outa here," Ely hissed to Ian.

"Sure you're not going to tell us where you caught all those fish?" said the fat man, writing fast.

"I guess not," Ian said.

"Handy here?"

"Not far."

"That's funny. That's really odd." The fat reporter

tipped back his hat, as all the brooks in the county ran through his head.

"Stream aint been fished since ninety," Ian cried suddenly in a high, squeaky voice, and everyone laughed good-naturedly.

At last the reporter let them go, and they wheeled home. Ian had to sit down for a while on the back steps with the basket between his knees because his legs wouldn't hold him up. At last he tottered into the kitchen and planked the basket down in the sink. His father was poking the fire. "What have you go there that's so heavy?" he said.

"Fish." Ian poured a drink of water.

His father looked at him hard, then walked over and lifted the cover.

"Well I swan," he said slowly. He turned toward the hall door. "Hey, Mother — Rufus! Come here quick."

It was the very next evening that B.J. came over to the house. "Rufus," he said abruptly, "I've been thinking over that proposition of yours."

Uncle Rufus jumped up as if a bee had stung him. "You come right into the parlor, B.J.," he said. "Wallace, you come too."

It was almost bedtime when the three brothers came out of the parlor. "Tell me now, B.J.," Rufus was saying, "what made you change your mind?"

"Well, I'll tell you, Rufus. I got families on my books that are two hundred dollars behind on their bills. I can't cut them off, because for years they were good customers, but if the men don't work soon, their families are going to eat me right out of business and into the poorhouse. So I figure I got no choice. I may be ruined by going into this shoe factory gamble, but I'll certainly be ruined if my customers don't get some work pretty soon."

"Is that the only reason?" Ian's father asked. "Because that situation hasn't come up overnight."

B.J. rubbed his chin, and as he did so his eye fell on Ian sitting at the kitchen table with his algebra problems. "You're right. I don't know what it was that made me change my mind unless it was those boys catching all those fish. I remember as I was walking home that night I kept saying to myself, You can't just let yourself slide over the bank like this, B.J. You got to do something — got to take a chance. And then I saw those kids with their fish. That's when the idea came to me that we were going to have to try the impossible — were going to have to *believe* in the impossible — just like those kids believed there were fish in that stream, when every single one of us grownups all swore there were no fish anywhere around here."

After B.J. went, Ian's father said to Uncle Rufus, "But, we're going to need more than B.J."

"Never mind, Wallace." Uncle Rufus was walking about slapping his fist into his palm. "It's started."

And started it had. The point was that B.J. had such a reputation for cautiousness in business matters that when people heard he was going to back the shoe factory they began to believe in it in spite of themselves. From that beginning, something passed through the town — a current of excitement. It changed people's faces. It even changed their dispositions. They brought out their lifetime hoardings, money they had been saving for their coffins. And Uncle Rufus was like a man waking up after a long sleep. He rushed about buzzing like a dynamo, inspiring enthusiasm everywhere.

Still, at the end of the second week they lacked five thousand dollars necessary for the absolute minimum to get the factory going. And there was no more capital to be found in the town. Some people had even cashed in their paid-up life insurance policies.

"It's no use," Uncle Rufus said at last, "we'll have to go to Father again. You call him up, Mabe." He turned to Ian's mother, "and tell him we need him."

Then in the middle of all the excitement Ian got the mumps. It was a mild attack, not much fever, but his mother put him to bed just the same.

On Thursday evening his mother insisted that everyone, his father and Uncle Rufus and herself, all go to prayer meeting. "It won't do a bit of harm to try a little prayer," she said. "I'll get someone to sit with Ian, just in case he needs something. I'll get the Manship girl down the street. Those people could certainly use a quarter."

He listened in amazement. Was it possible that she didn't know about the Manship girl? He lay very still, his body all creepy under the covers at the thought of being alone in the house with that splendid, bad girl.

In the evening after supper he heard them dressing, and at seven o'clock he heard the front doorbell ring and then his mother's bell-like voice and then a lower, softer, girl's voice — a strangely exciting sound in his own house. "He's in the room at the end of the hall," his mother said. "I don't think he'll need anything, but I didn't like to leave him alone. You've had the mumps I suppose."

Again that low, thrilling voice sounded — husky and soft — full of unmentionable promises.

"You'll find plenty to read. Ian's room is full of books. He's a great reader — "

The voices faded. He heard the door open and close again and then his mother talking to his father outside as they went down the walk.

For a few minutes the house was still. She's hanging up her coat, he thought. Then he heard quick, light steps on the stairs.

She stood framed in the doorway, her smooth face glowing warmly in the light of the lamp, her garnet lips curling at the corners in a slow grin — the blue-black eyes burning at him.

"Hello," she said, her voice expressionless.

"Hello," he muttered.

She walked over to the chair, stopping to pick up a book from the little pile on the table. She sat down, crossing her legs and opening the book. He stole quick glances at her long, shapely legs and the sweet curve of her cheek below the silky lashes. He pretended to read his own book, but the lines were a mere blur. He lay tense under the covers, the blood pounding through his veins. It was incredible that she should be alone with him in the empty house, in his very bedroom. The room seemed to grow quieter and quieter, until he could hear the watch ticking on the stand by his bed. Somehow he knew that she wasn't reading her book any more than he was reading his. The room seemed filled with some strange kind of electricity. Something was going to happen. He didn't know what. He had never been alone in a house with a girl before.

Suddenly she closed her book with a little clap of sound. He jumped and looked up, startled. She leaned back in the chair, stretching her arms over her head languidly so that her breasts swelled against her blouse. Her eyes were inscrutable under their lashes. "Do you really like to read?" she asked. "I think books are mighty dull."

He mumbled something. He didn't know what.

"Not nearly so exciting as the real thing." She brought her arms down, smoothing her skirt over her thighs. She got up and walked around the room, pretending to look at the pictures on the walls. Then abruptly she turned about and faced him at the side of the bed. "You're kind of a pretty boy," she said.

He stared at her — a bird watching a glittering serpent — full of a sweet fear.

Slowly, graceful as a cat, she sat down on the edge of the bed. "Isn't there something we can do?" she shook her thick black bob. Her hot eyes watched his mouth.

He ran his tongue over his lips. "What?" he whispered.

Her eyes stayed on his mouth. "Don't you know what?"

It was incredible — like a dream. "N-n-no." His teeth chattered.

The red mouth curled. He saw her face through a haze, soft and glowing, so beautiful that he felt sick with longing. It was the color of a rose in sunlight. Her dark eyes were two blackbirds nesting in the rose of her face. "Do you want me to show you?" She spoke slowly, languidly, her lips parted.

His pulse leaped. He stared up into her bright, sinful eyes. For a long time the word hung on his lips, the silence glowing. She played with one of the little knots on the quilt.

"Yes," he whispered at last.

"Do you really?" Her arms went to the back of her blouse, deftly undoing the buttons. She arched her waist slightly and the blouse slipped away from the delicate shoulders. She leaned forward a little and it fell away from her.

He lay helpless looking at the smooth globes of her breasts, drooping a little as she bent toward him.

Her flushed face came down over him, the dark hair falling across her mouth. Her smooth cheek brushed lightly against his, hot as fire. "You can feel them if you want to," she whispered.

The honeyed sin of her voice poured over him. He put out his hand and touched that smooth, heavy, yielding fruit, smoother than anything his fingers had ever touched before, smoother than any imagined smoothness. Instinctively his hand cupped this wonderful thing. The little nipple rose under his hand.

"Stop that!" she whispered, her voice like a velvet whip, but her cheek slid slowly back and forth against his, and her hand crept up around his neck. And at that moment, as from a tremendous distance, he heard his mother's clear, golden voice coming through the window. He twisted his face away. "My mother!" he cried softly.

She sat up quickly, her eyes very odd, more like some startled animal's eyes than human eyes. Quickly she jumped up from the bed and began feverishly buttoning up her blouse. "God damn!" she said softly.

The door downstairs opened, and his mother called up cheerily. "Everything all right up there?"

Sweetly innocent, Molly's voice floated down. "Yes, Mrs. McAleenan." Her face, bent over a little as she stuffed her blouse into her skirt, was a flaming red.

When his mother entered the room, she was sitting sedately in the chair again, just closing her book.

"Prayer meeting was short tonight," his mother said. "I brought you some ice cream." She held out the two dishes.

"Oh I couldn't," said Molly politely.

Ian stared at her, astonished at such smooth hypocrisy.

As she set the dish down in front of him, his mother put her cool hand on his forehead. "You've still got some fever," she said. "The ice cream will be good for it."

She went over to the door. "I'll eat mine with Father. When you're through, Molly, come down and I'll pay you." She smiled at them gently and went out of the room.

They sat spooning their ice cream. It was the first time he had ever eaten ice cream without tasting it.

"That was a close call," she said. She stood up with her empty dish in her hand. For a long moment they just looked at each other; her eyes were unfathomable shadows under her thick lashes. Then suddenly she was gone.

The next day he was well again and went off to school. It was on the way home that he saw her coming along the street toward him, her mop of black hair tossing about her pretty face. He grew tense. What would they say to each other? Would he — would he dare —

A lazy smile curled the red lips as she came up to him. "Hello, kid," she said coolly. The blowtorches flickered briefly over him and she passed on.

7

IT WAS THE last week of school, and there was going to be a school dance. In the corridors and cloakrooms the dance was all they talked about. The ability to dance suddenly became the most precious of accomplishments. There was much talk about two-steps, one-steps, fox-trotting, gliding, and it was all Greek to Ian, for he had just discovered a horrible flaw in his personality — he didn't know how to dance. To make matters worse Peebles had become insufferably superior, claiming to have mastered the gentle art during a visit to a girl cousin's. He offered to teach Ian, but since he didn't know how to go backward, it was no good.

He was too proud to tell his troubles to anyone but Peebles and his mother, but his mother must have told Mrs. Antonelli, for when there were only three days left before the dance, she stopped him in the yard, looking at him out of her sympathetic eyes.

"Tonight we are having the spaghetti," she said. "Do you want to come and help us eat it?" The corners of her full mouth crinkled.

"You bet." He smiled into her eyes.

"Afterwards we will have a little music on the phonograph, and you and Francesca will dance. Francesca dances beautifully. She has a natural talent for dancing." She spread her hands softly. "No?"

"But *I* can't dance at all," he said.

"All the better. Francesca will teach you."

Thus it happened that for the next three nights he went over to the Antonellis' and danced around the parlor to the sound of the phonograph, with the slender Francesca swaying like a reed in his arms. He was surprised how easy it was. Francesca was very patient, smiling at him when his clumsy feet bumped against hers. He thought it was too bad Francesca wasn't coming to the school dance, but Francesca went to the Parish School.

The night of the dance he was too excited to eat much supper, and rushed upstairs right after dessert to get dressed. For a long time he stood in front of the mirror over the washbasin studying the reflection of his face. He didn't look too bad in this mirror, but in his bedroom mirror he looked horrible. In his bedroom mirror the place where he had the back tooth taken out looked like a big hole in the side of his cheek. Sometimes he kept a wad of gum up there to fill in the hollow. But in the bathroom mirror he looked almost handsome. He pulled his comb out and tried combing his hair straight back. He turned his head sideways trying to see his profile, but it always got away from him at the last moment. He wondered if his nose was too long, and suddenly to his horror he noticed on his cheek, down near his ear, a large, white-headed pimple. He looked at it appalled. What a horrible thing. He squeezed it viciously. Back in his bedroom putting on his shirt, he took one quick look at himself in the bedroom mirror and quailed.

Peebles came for him at a quarter to eight. He was wearing a bow tie, and it seemed to have gone to his head. He didn't seem like the old Peebles at all — didn't talk like him. They sat down in the parlor and watched the hands of the green marble clock. When it was eight-thirty, Ian jumped up, but Peebles looked at him scornfully. "Ya never go to these things on time," he said. "We gotta wait another half an hour at least."

As they walked down Church Street, Ian kept saying under his breath, "I'll ask her if it kills me. I'll walk right up to her and say, 'Hyah, Adrienne — this one taken?' "

"Never ask em if this one is taken," said Peebles suddenly. "Ya always say, 'Mind if I have this one?' or 'Care to dance?' "

They came to the Armory, where the dance was being held, an enormous, bleak sandstone building with two crenellated towers. They walked through the arched doorway and joined the little crowd of boys hanging close to the entry in a tight, jostling clump, as if they were all afraid the place might catch fire or something.

Since the drill floor of the armory was too large, a square

of benches had been set up in the center, over which hung festoons of red and white tissue paper, with a number of red and white balloons hanging on strings.

A few girls were already seated on the benches, clustering together and leaning toward each other. Every once in a while two or three more girls came in through the entry, hurrying through the barrier of boys haughtily. The boys stared at them with stiff shoulders and blank faces, as if they were some strange species of fish sailing past them. All of the boys looked very proud and stern, as if they had just been secretly challenged to a duel. Only the closest friends broke this frozen appearance with a fleeting smile.

Presently, with a great deal of tuning and testing, the three-piece orchestra, a drum, a violin and a saxophone, started playing a fox trot, and immediately Ian felt a ripple of excitement run through the crowd of boys around him. He could feel it himself. But in spite of the excitement it produced no further effect than a lot of neck-craning, as the boys picked out the girl they would dance with if they had the nerve to walk across the bare expanse of floor and ask her. Just suppose she refused you, and you had to walk all the way back with every single person in the room watching you. There was a thought to halt the bravest.

At last, when it seemed that the orchestra was going to have to be satisfied to give a concert, the boy beside Ian gave a convulsive jerk, straightened his tie, coughed, and said in the tone of one walking up to the guillotine, "Well, here goes," and shot swiftly across the open floor as if it were thin ice at a pace that wasn't exactly a run, but was more than a walk.

Ian watched the unknown hero with awe as he went up to one of the girls, bowed, and led her out onto the floor.

After that it was apparently much easier, for half a dozen other daredevils managed to take the irrevocable step, and soon they were moving slowly or rapidly about the room with their partners. Eventually Peebles, who had been twitching and hunching like a boy with St. Vitus's dance, gave a sort of shiver and walked out toward the benches very much as if he were sleepwalking. Ian followed him with his eyes, saw him bend over a girl in a green dress and take her out onto the floor. He thought Peebles didn't look so hot for one who pretended to be a master of the dance. He stumbled a good deal and seemed to by trying all the time to see his feet over the girl's shoulder.

All in all about three quarters of the boys didn't take any chances at all, but stuck close to the entrance, and Ian was among them. Try as he would, he just couldn't get his feet to take him out across the empty space between him and those girls. Suddenly, as he stood there sweating and cursing himself for a miserable coward, he heard a bright little cascade of girl laughter behind him, and one of those voices was familiar. In a panic he ducked swiftly behind the nearest boy and peered around his shoulder. It was Adrienne all right. He caught his breath, and a sharp pain seemed to hit him in the chest as she passed so close to him, her black reefer thrown over her shoulder like a wrap, and a snowy white dress gleaming underneath, her polished black hair nestling in soft curls on the collar of her reefer, her dark eyes dancing. He knew then and there that he would never have the nerve to walk up to such a heavenly creature and ask her to dance with such a crude, clumsy, ugly animal as himself. His evening was now ruined. He might as well go home.

He looked out at Peebles and felt a sick pang of envy. Peebles was no longer looking at his partner's feet. He was swinging her around like a veteran, his arm holding the girl's out straight and going up and down as if he were pumping a well, his rear end wiggling like a dog's shaking off water, and when his face came around, the look of smugness, with the mouth pursed and the eyes cast upward and his head tossing and nodding, was utterly unbearable.

And all the while he, Ian, stood among the cravens, safe and miserable all through the first half of the dance. It was hard to tell which moment was more miserable than another, but nothing was worse than the time he saw Peebles dancing with Adrienne. There was just one consolation for the boys at the entrance. At intermission time they were suddenly in a position of strategic advantage, with the big trays of ice cream and cake having to pass through them before they could get out onto the floor at all. Now they took their revenge on that happy group by sweeping the trays bare like a flock of ravenous vultures. They ate ice cream so fast they choked, got red in the face and teary-eyed, and grabbed another dish. The cravens became gluttons and drowned their misery in food.

After the intermission the orchestra started up again with renewed vigor, and the whole dreary spectacle began all over again. Ian stood as if rooted, impulse throbbing in every artery, hating his cowardly self as if he were his deadliest enemy. A kind of monstrous crisis was growing in him, a desperate, concentrated fury of suspended motion. He knew it was now or never, and suddenly, as if propelled from a gun, he found himself somehow rushing across the floor directly at little Erminie Van Epps, who just happened to be sitting on the corner of the bench nearest to him.

He was standing in front of her, flushed and throbbing. She looked up at him out of startled, frightened eyes, and in those eyes he read NO in capital letters, but he never let the word materialize. "C'n I have this one?" he shouted, and grabbed for her hand.

The wild look in his eyes must have hypnotized her, for she stood up without a murmur.

He had picked out Erminie because he knew her, not because she was an ideal partner for him. When she stood up, she came only to the second button of his jacket. To take hold of her arm and put his own around her waist, he had to bend away over until his ear touched her cheek and his backside stuck out at a sharp angle. She put one hand light as a feather on his shoulder, and so they ventured out onto the dangerous sea of the dance floor. He seemed immediately to have forgotten everything he had learned about dancing. Every place he went to put his feet, Erminie's little foot was sure to be there first. Once he stepped right on the top of her toe, and she uttered a little gasp. He was in too great an agony even to apologize, for now he was learning that there was a torture far worse than being frozen in that group of ne'er-do-wells around the entry.

In the midst of the ordeal, when he was at his very worst, the perspiration streaming down his face, his eyes a nest of pain, he found himself looking directly into the face of Adrienne, her cheek nestled against the cheek of some strange boy, a little smile hovering about her mouth, her eyes closed blissfully. He swung little Erminie around so violently that she almost fell, and he almost ran with her across the floor to get away from that dangerous vision.

When it was over, they walked silently back to the benches, and because there didn't seem to be anything else to do, he sat down beside her. But they had nothing to say to each other; they sat locked in their own misery. He thought: So I can't dance after all. I shall never again in my whole life have the nerve to ask another girl to go through such a thing.

He waited for someone to take Erminie away so he could sneak off home. He knew when he was beaten. He felt that he had grown old and gray in one evening.

Someone sat down beside him and nudged him in the ribs. He turned and looked into the sweaty shining face of Peebles. "Some dance, eh." Peebles spoke breezily, wiping his neck with his handkerchief. "Nice little orchestra."

Ian stared at him. "Yeah," he muttered, "pretty good."

Peebles turned easily to the girl on the other side of him, bending his head solicitously.

Somewhere a boy stood up with a megaphone to his mouth. "The next dance," he called out, "will be girl's choice. Go get em, girls."

There was a murmur of giggling and whispering. The orchestra began a waltz, and the brave girls were almost at once running this way and that for their partners. They were far, far braver then the boys. It was an amazing thing to discover. They laughed at danger. He watched them numbly. After his performance with Erminie, which he was sure no eye in the hall had missed, one thing was certain, no girl was going to ask *him* to dance. But all at once his heart took a violent somersault. Who was that coming across the floor, swaying slightly in her white dress, her proud little head half turned sideways like some lovely flower? Who but Adrienne — a vision so divine that his eyes went all blurry. She wasn't looking at him, but she was coming right toward him. He watched her, mesmerized. Straight as an arrow she came toward him. Suddenly she was standing in front of him. The blood rushed to his head; he couldn't see, he couldn't hear. He started to rise. Then he saw that she wasn't looking at him. She was looking at somebody beside him, and he remembered unbelievingly, that Peebles was still there. She was asking *Peebles.*

He was a boy of burnt-out ashes sitting there on the bench as they danced away. He didn't know what was keeping him upright, when he should have been a heap on the floor.

"Excuse me," said Erminie, standing up. She walked away to ask someone else to dance.

He was left alone. The whole length of the benches was empty except for one other sheepish, uncomfortable-looking boy. They eyed each other and looked away. He wondered what horrible obnoxiousness resided in the other boy. There they were, the two sole pariahs. It was a mortification too great to bear. He looked toward the entry, girding his loins to make the ignominious dash back to anonymity.

"May I have this dance with you?" Fine and clear, the sweet voice floated down upon him.

But he didn't bother to look up. He knew the improbable when he heard it. He was imagining that clear and lovely voice. Yet there was the little gold slipper peeping out beneath the black silk skirt. He looked up. A slender, russet-cheeked girl was looking down at him, her small face tilted proudly, as if she would turn away at once if he didn't very quickly and gratefully accept the honor she was bestowing on him. He stared at the two little laughter dimples at each corner of her mouth, and then into the long, gray, tapering eyes.

He looked at her so long that she put her hand up to her hair and bit her lip. At that little gesture he leaped to his feet like a jack-in-the-box. He reached out his hand, their fingers interlocked, her arm came up over his shoulder and lightly around his neck. They took a step together, and she yielded miraculously, as if she weren't there at all for a moment, as if they were one person. The music soared. They moved out onto the floor. Body and soul, he danced — lost in music, motion, and sweetest union. A kind of shiver passed through his body, and all his cares and tension dropped away. It was as if he had been dancing all his life, it was so easy and natural with this girl. He swung her around slowly. She glanced up at him, her eyes narrowing into a smile. He slipped his hand a little farther about her waist, and in one perfect moment of time her smooth cheek touched his and rested there. He closed his eyes. Once her voice sounded at his ear. "You dance nicely."

"*You're* a *wonderful* dancer," he breathed.

When the music stopped, they moved easily through the couples. He was at peace with the world again. He stole quick glances at her. What a strange girl she was, so poised. He had a slightly eerie feeling, as if she wasn't real. A little breathless turmoil seemed to hover about her, a delicate swirl of magic in the air. Their eyes crossed. "It's funny I never saw you anywhere before," he said.

She smiled, and he watched, fascinated at the way her lips curled so perfectly, the dimples coming and going. "Oh I just came down out the sky."

He almost believed her. "Where *do* you live?" he insisted.

"I told you — in the sky. And when the dance is over, I'm going back again."

His heart ached. She must be visiting someone. When the dance was over, he would never see her again. His mouth trembled. A tremendous daring filled him. He swallowed. "May I take you home?" he said.

Her long eyes mused on his face. "Do you know how to fly?" Her lips trembled. She giggled.

The music started, and they began to dance again. Her

voice came low and oddly serious at his ear. "Do you mean you want the last dance?"

"Yes." He thought his heart would burst.

"All right." They danced on. "But I don't know whether you can take me home or not. I'll tell you when the last dance comes."

He left her at last with two older girls whom he didn't know and strolled with a little swagger over toward the sad-eyed bachelors at the entry. Poor fellows. They weren't having much fun. Too bad they didn't know how easy it was. He shouldered his way through them haughtily. But outside, in the cool night alone, the haughtiness all left him. He looked up at the stars. He wanted to thank someone for being alive.

Behind him the music started up again, but he didn't go in. He didn't want to dance with anyone else but her. Even though he knew he could walk up to any girl in the room, even Adrienne. After a while, he went in and stood in the entry. He saw the strange girl dancing with someone else. It didn't bother him. She had given *him* the last dance. That meant for sure a girl liked you best. Still he didn't want *her* to see him standing there, so he went back into the shadows of the archway.

Finally the boy with the megaphone announced that most sacred of all dances — the good-night waltz. Now would those intended to be together be seen together. His breath came quickly. He waited until two or three couples were swaying dreamily, before he walked over to her. She rose at once, smiling. They floated away together. They didn't talk. Once in a while her cheek brushed against his, and then stayed. And then it was as if the music wound them around and around, closer and closer together. "Someone is taking the girl I came with," she murmured, "so I guess *you'll* have to take *me*."

He didn't answer, just held her a little tighter. She seemed to understand, because she didn't say anything more.

When it was at last over, they stood with the others and clapped wildly. Then she flashed him a bright glance and told him to wait for her at the entrance while she got her coat.

As she came toward him, tall and slim in a dark red coat, he was so proud that his chest swelled against the buttons of his jacket. He saw Peebles step forward and take the arm of a girl. To his surprise it was Adrienne. He hadn't even looked for her once in the last half hour. For a moment they were all together in a little huddle. "Hello, you old son of a gun," he said loudly to Peebles and gave him a resounding slap between his thin shoulder blades. "Some dance, hey!"

Peebles was staring at the girl beside him, his eyebrows making question marks on his forehead. Ian glanced at Adrienne. She was looking at the strange girl too, but her face was completely inscrutable. He knew that he should introduce the girl he was with, but realized all at once that he didn't even know her name. "See you tomorrow," he said to Peebles, and tapping a shoulder in front of him, he said in his most condescending voice, "May we pass, please." He thought there was just a little bit of awe in the boy's eyes as he stepped back.

They walked slowly through the dark streets. They didn't say much, but it was enough. He asked her her name, and she said it was Irene. Now that they were alone, a kind of terrible, bitter-sweet constraint was upon them. They moved through an invisible, poignant melancholy. He wondered if she felt, as he did, that they might never see each other again. Finally, she stopped before a house.

"This is where I'm staying," she said.

He moved up the walk with her. She stood quietly by the door facing him, but with her head a little to one side. In the dim light her face was so perfectly beautiful and desirable that he held his breath. He wanted terribly to kiss her, but he couldn't move. He wanted to say something that would keep her there, but he couldn't think of anything. The silence grew with merciless insistence. She moved her head, looked up at the stars, then directly into his face, and there was something sad and almost accusing in that tense and direct look. Her gray eyes seemed almost black in the shadow of her lashes, and the corners of her mouth drooped. He knew. He knew what he should do. But he had never done it before. He could feel his hand trembling.

She made a slight movement to take hold of the doorknob, and a little rueful smile played over her mouth. "Good night," she said and turned the knob of the door.

"Wait!" His voice sounded in his ears like the croak of a dying frog.

She waited.

But he couldn't move, and he couldn't speak. A terrible sinking feeling passed through him. There was no longer any doubt. He was a craven coward, a hopeless craven coward. *She* was the one who had asked him to dance. *He* had done nothing. What despising thoughts she must have about him. She was probably thinking right now about what a mistake she had made asking *him* to dance with her, letting *him* take her home, when there were lots of other guys who knew what to do when they were saying good night to a pretty girl.

But at that moment, cutting sharply across his thoughts, came from the shadowy side of the house a sound like a soul shrieking in hell. So loud and shrill and unexpected was it that she jumped half laughing, half frightened, holding his arm and leaning against him.

"It's only an old tomcat," he said and stopped. Her very clear gray eyes were so close and so bright and were looking at him in such a special intense, questioning way that he suddenly couldn't breathe. He felt his head going forward. He shut his eyes. His mouth found hers blindly in the darkness, and the sweetness at the core of life flooded through all the rivers of his being, and he would never be the same again.

When the age of time that was the length of their kiss had passed, and they were partially separate beings again, but not completely, still sweetly intimate, touching each other, looking at each other like discoverers of rich new lands, serious eyed, she suddenly squeezed his fingers gently. "Good night," she said softly. "And pleasant dreams." She opened the door quickly and went in.

As he walked down the path, a black cat with a soft, purring moan slipped past his feet. In the shadows the brindle tom watched both him and the black cat. "Hyah, boy," he said to the tom.

He turned up the street. It was absolutely still and warm, the air sweet with the perfume of early roses. One by one the dim street lights picked him up and let him go. He walked along absently, hugging his joy, hardly conscious of where he put his feet, turning automatically at the right corners, whistling a little tune. And far, far above those feeble street lights, safely remote in the velvet darkness of the night, the great thermo-nuclear furnaces of the stars blazed and roared to fuse the elements to make possible such throbbing joy in one gangling adolescent boy, whose trousers, already twice let down by his mother, were once again too short for him.

Later, in bed, it seemed to him that he had at last only fallen asleep when he woke up with a start. It was still pitch-dark, but the house was as full of noise as a house could be without falling apart. His father was chopping kindlings fiercely in the shed, but outside, rising high above the chopping, came a tremendous banging, as if someone were beating a frying pan with a sledgehammer. He crawled out of bed, pulled on his pants and stumbled downstairs. The kitchen clock said four-thirty. His father was rattling the stove lids, and as Ian stepped into the kitchen, who should stamp in through the back door, slamming it behind him, but his Grandfather McAleenan.

"Flat tire," he said. "These city streets full of nails."

Ian peered at him out of sleepy eyes, while the two men bustled around him as if he were a post in the middle of the kitchen. His grandfather put something into his hands and said something to him, but he was too sleepy to understand what. After a while his grandfather came back and took the bundle out of his hands again.

Soon his mother came down and made breakfast, but his grandfather would eat nothing but piece after piece of bread. "Haven't had a piece of store bread in over a year," he said, breaking the bread up into little pieces and pushing them into his mouth one after the other. "Tastes good." His face was long and hollow-cheeked, the skin the color of old brass, shiny over the cheekbones, and as he ate, his black beard bobbed up and down rhythmically, and his clear blue eyes moved continuously over their faces and around the room, never still for a second.

When breakfast was over, his grandfather wiped his beard carefully with his napkin and let out two buttons of his black vest.

Uncle Rufus cleared his throat. "Wallace and I want to talk to you about something, Father."

The old man darted him a quick look. "Must be about money, you're in such a hurry. Only money makes people hurry."

Uncle Rufus shifted uncomfortably in his chair.

"The root of all evil." The blue eyes were regarding Ian. They weren't stern and they weren't laughing.

"Now you know you don't believe that," Ian's father said. "You always taught us to be thrifty. Money means hard work, thrift, responsibility, self-denial and good sense — all good things."

"Also greed. 'Do not worship Mammon,' the Bible says."

"Nobody here worships it, Father." Uncle Rufus was quite red in the face.

"Well, well. We'll talk about it later. Now I'll just have a little nap, and then young Ian and I will take a look at the town. Don't get to town every day, you know." He stood up, and Ian's mother led him into the parlor, where he stretched out on the couch. Ian looked at him from the door as he lay slim and small and serene in his snowy shirt and black vest. He could smell him in the parlor. He smelled like apples and dried leaves and fresh-cut wood.

His mother took him by the arm. "Be very quiet," she said, drawing him out of the kitchen. "He must be tired after his long drive." Her face was tender. She spoke softly.

"It isn't going to be easy," Uncle Rufus was saying. "He always had a stubborn will, you know."

Ian's father sat hunched over the table, running the tips of his fingers over his mustache, over and over. "It's hopeless," he said. "He belongs to another time. He doesn't understand investment. He thinks money is to be saved in a teapot for a rainy day. Three per cent he thinks is plenty — more is sinful."

"Your father is a very smart man," Ian's mother said.

His father grinned at her. "You always had a soft spot in your heart for him." His hand tightened on the table. "I'd never be able to face him, if we lost his money."

"It's the chance you take," Uncle Rufus said grimly.

It was almost an hour before his grandfather came walking into the kitchen, his blue eyes brighter than ever, his back straight as a spruce tree. "Now we'll see what's going on in the city," he said.

Ian grinned at hearing the town called a city. He stood up. He knew his grandfather meant they should go together.

"I'll just drop over and say hello to Basil," his grandfather said, and it wasn't until they entered the grocery store that Ian realized he had meant B.J.

"I'll have ten cents' worth of those peppermints," his grandfather said to B.J., and B.J. looked up and almost ran around the counter to shake hands. He scooped out a big bagful of peppermints, much more than ten cents' worth and tried to wave away the dime the old man held out. "Now, Father," he protested.

"Business is business," said his grandfather. "I always made you boys earn whatever you got from me, and now I expect to pay for whatever I get from you. That's the way I want it."

B.J. took the dime. His grandfather held out the bag to Ian, stuffed a peppermint into his own mouth and put the rest carefully away in his pocket. "Now let's see what's going on," he said.

They walked up Church Street. Opposite the Blue Moon Grill his grandfather saw a big plate of bananas in the window. "Bananas!" he said. "I'll have to have some of those."

"They don't sell things in there," Ian said. "That's a restaurant."

"They'll sell em to me," said his grandfather firmly and strode into the restaurant. "I'd like three pounds of those bananas," he said to the man standing behind the register.

The man frowned. "Not for sale, old chap. What do you think this is, a grocery store?"

Ian flushed to hear anyone talk to his grandfather that way.

But his grandfather just grinned. "Now, now, John Berry, your daddy never taught you to talk this way to your elders."

The man stared into his face for a moment before the cross look began to disappear.

"Trouble is you're so busy trying to make money here that you don't have time to be polite."

The frown started to come back, and the man looked down the length of the restaurant as if there were something important he ought to be doing.

"Not much like your daddy. He couldn't make money at anything, but he always had a cheerful smile for everybody." His grandfather leaned easily on the counter. "Why I remember," he said, "your daddy had the only sweet pear tree in the county, and every fall he sent me a big bag of those pears."

The man behind the counter turned sharply. "Why Mr. McAleenan," he said, "I should have recognized you."

"Tut tut. A man changes with the years." His grandfather pulled his beard slowly.

"Now how many bananas did you want, Mr. McAleenan?" The man was already reaching under the counter for a paper bag.

"I usually buy about three pounds."

Outside again, his grandfather tucked the big bag of

bananas under his arm, chuckling. "Always like to get bananas when I come to town. Remember the first one I ever ate. Tried to eat it like an apple, bit right through the skin." He gave a little cackle.

Ian was curious. "It was funny he gave you the bananas for nothing," he said.

"I'll tell you. I had a mortgage on the old Berry place for years, and every fall when it came time to pay the interest, they always sent me a bag of pears instead." He smiled into Ian's eyes. "They meant all right. They just couldn't hold on to money." His grandfather started to walk along the sidewalk. "Now his son gives me bananas."

There was a shiny new Chevrolet parked across the street. His grandfather went over and walked around and around it. "All closed in," he said. "I wouldn't like that. No air." He reached in and tried the horn, smiled, and tried it again. "Sounds like a sick cow," he said cheerfully. He tapped the fenders with his knuckles. "Kind of tinny." Ian wondered if he was going to buy a new car, he was spending so much time. Suddenly, however, he started off rapidly up the street. Ian had to hurry to keep beside him.

They went into the hardware store, where his grandfather asked to see some pitchforks. He tried every pitchfork in the store, holding them with both hands and making vicious jabs so that the clerk moved cautiously out of range. "Don't just feel right, any of them," he said. "Don't see why they can't make a good pitchfork any more." He walked out of the store without buying any.

He stood for a long time on the corner by Fuller's Drugstore, just watching the people go by, his head moving back and forth, back and forth. Everyone turned to look at him as they passed, some even turned around to take a second glance, but he didn't seem to notice. "All these people walking around on a fine day like this," he said at last. "You don't see people walking around doing nothing on a fine day in the country. It looks bad — not what the Lord intended." He shook his head.

"There's no work for them to do," Ian blurted out. "They used to work in the shoe factory, but now it doesn't run any more."

"They can always grow food."

"They don't own any land. If the shoe factory doesn't run, there's nothing for them to do."

His grandfather gave him a long look, with one eyebrow up and the other down. "Come on," he said abruptly, "let's go home."

Going back down Church Street he said, "The town looks seedy. Like to see a place kept spruce. Same for a town as a farm. Can always tell a man from his buildings. A little white paint is all that's necessary."

"The people have no money for paint," Ian said. "They got no money for anything."

His grandfather walked faster.

When they came to the house, his grandfather started to turn into the drive and stopped. "Let's you and I just step around the corner and take a look at Rufus' old factory," he said.

He stood for a long time looking up at the factory. "Got a heap of broken windows," he said. "Windows and

boys — like apples and worms. They gotta make holes in em." He turned sharply on Ian. "You break any of those windows?"

Ian's eyes met the clear blue ones. "One," he said.

When they got to the house, his grandfather squeezed himself between the kitchen stove and the hot-water tank. "Now boys," he said to Uncle Rufus and Ian's father, "what have you got up your sleeves?"

Uncle Rufus cleared his throat and began to talk. As he talked, Ian's grandfather kept tossing peppermints into his mouth. Finally Uncle Rufus leaned back and said, "And that's it. That's the story. We've got to have five thousand more."

"Well, boys." His grandfather munched away. "You think I got about twenty thousand dollars. I might as well tell you I got fifteen thousand dollars all tied up in mortgages on farms."

Ian's father jumped up. "Great Scot!" he cried. "You couldn't sell a farm around here today for a song."

His grandfather peered into the peppermint bag. "I guess you're right. Some of em's paying interest and some aren't."

"Well that's awful," said Uncle Rufus, "just awful. The way they've taken advantage of you, dumping their run-down old farms in your lap, taking the money you've worked so hard all your life to earn — worked while they loafed."

His grandfather tossed another peppermint into his mouth. "Wasn't exactly their fault. Those were good farms — still are. All at once there wasn't any money in farming. They come to me with their sad tale — boys I went to school with in that little school at the Corners, boys I sat beside in the old church for years. I just couldn't say no to them. You see —" The blue eyes grew vague. "I was trying to save the whole community — my way of life —" His grandfather shot them a look from under his brows. "I've barely got five thousand dollars left."

There was a little silence. Then Uncle Rufus sighed and stood up heavily. "*We* are trying to save a *town*," he said, "but I'm not going to ask you for your last five thousand dollars."

The old man crumpled up the little brown bag. The last peppermint was gone. "You don't need to ask me, Rufus. I'm giving it to you anyway."

Ian was up in his room. He had a wonderful feeling. School was over and a whole long wonderful summer evening stretched away ahead of him with no lessons. Through the open window he could hear familiar voices, among them the clear laughing girl voice of Francesca Antonelli. Last week Francesca began combing her hair back and tying it with a ribbon, and suddenly she was beautiful. The world was full of such surprises. Her face had come out of the bush of her hair like a pure, clean-lined cameo, with enormous black, speaking eyes. He peered at himself in the mirror twisting his head this way and that, trying to outwit the mirror's trick of making his face so long, and at that moment a strange new sound filled the air — the shoe factory whistle. Long and loud and gaily it blew — on and on. He stood with his brush and comb in his hand listening.

A little later the street was full of the boisterous sound of men's voices as the workmen came up from the factory, and in a moment Uncle Rufus and his father came bustling in. Uncle Rufus' hat was tipped back on his head the way he used to wear it, and under his arm was a roll of blue-prints. His father was laughing.

"And this machine," Uncle Rufus was saying, "we found in the old packing room. I have never seen anything like it before, I swear, not in all my years of shoe manufacturing. You can shoot me if I ever remember it."

Ian grew tense. When they had learned that the shoe

factory was going to open again, they had dismantled their gymnasium, but they had left the old treadmill. It hadn't worked anyway.

"For a while," Uncle Rufus went on, "none of us could figure it out. Then one of the men came in and said it was an old-style leather soaker. He said he had seen lots of them in the old country. Seemed to know all about it."

"Well, well," his father said. They hung their hats on the rack and went into the parlor.

From the kitchen came his mother's voice. "For heaven's sake! We've eaten long ago."

"We had a lot to do," Uncle Rufus replied.

Ian came down the stairs. Through the parlor door he could see them. Uncle Rufus had the blueprints spread all over the big table, and he and Ian's father were already bent over them, their heads close together. He went on out the front door.

Peebles was waiting for him on the steps. Ian sat down beside him, and for a little while a very curious thing happened — they couldn't think of anything to do. It was already too dark for baseball.

Then the Antonelli screen door slammed and out came Francesca again and with her Adrienne. They stood for a moment undecided on the walk and then, ping, ping, ping, all the way down the street the little stars of the street lights went on. Suddenly, there was soft laughter from the girls, and very low, but very clear and unmistakable came a voice: "Come on over."

Ian looked at Peebles. "What are we waiting for?" he said.